I0790938

The Mankeeper

The Mankeeper

Suzanne Visser

CONTENTS

Mankeeping Is Why Women Are Done With Dating

Researchers at Stanford University have finally given a name to something many women have been dealing with for years. It's called mankeeping. And it's helping explain why so many women are stepping away from dating altogether.

Mankeeping describes the emotional labour women end up doing in heterosexual relationships. It goes beyond remembering birthdays or coordinating social plans. It means being your partner's one-man support system. Managing his stress. Interpreting his moods. Holding his hand through feelings he won't share with anyone else. All of it unpaid, unacknowledged, and often unreciprocated.

The root of the issue is tied to what experts are calling the male loneliness epidemic. As more men report having fewer close friendships, romantic partners are expected to pick up the slack. Instead of processing with friends, many men offload everything onto the woman they're dating. She becomes his entire emotional infrastructure.

Plenty of women are no longer interested in that dynamic. According to *Pew Research*, only 38 per cent of single women in the US are currently looking for a relationship. Among single men, that number jumps to 61 per cent. The gap says a lot. Women aren't opting out of love. They're opting out of being someone's therapist with benefits.

The Guardian calls mankeeping a modern extension of emotional labour, one that turns a partner into a life coach. This isn't about avoiding vulnerability. It's about refusing to carry someone else's emotional weight while getting little to nothing in return. And there's nothing wrong with feeling that way.

Some men have started opening up more, which is good. But too often, that openness lands in the lap of the person they're sleeping with instead of a friend or a therapist. Vulnerability without boundaries can feel more like a burden than a breakthrough.

What women want isn't complicated. They want shared effort. Mutual support. Emotional responsibility that doesn't get passed off like a group project. When that doesn't happen, they're choosing solitude over stress. And they're not apologising for it.

Some women are called bitter for stepping back from dating. Others are labelled cold. What they're really doing is protecting their capacity. The choice to stay single rarely comes from defeat. It comes from knowing exactly how much energy they have left to give. Until that imbalance shifts, more women will keep walking away. Being alone is easier than managing someone else's emotional life.

Ashley Fike, June 20, 2025, VICE. https://www.vice.com/en/article/mankeeping-is-why-women-are-done-with-dating/

Part I SUMMER

The New Word

At seventy-nine, Joy has a new job title. It sits under her skin like a splinter: *Mankeeper.* She learned this word yesterday and knows it fits her like a glove. No, she's not dressing him, not bathing him. Yet. Those will come later, winter weather promised in the forecast. He's not sick. She is not a carer. *He's just old.*

For now, it is the invisible work that takes her breath. She reads his face the way farmers look at the sky and decide on the day. High cloud means caution. A heat haze means slowness. A crisp blue can still deliver a gust that knocks a person sideways. She keeps the kettle ready and the voice she uses for mornings, a shade brighter than her own.

The house carries the habits of their marriage. Shoes aligned by the back door. Tea towels folded precisely, one on the oven rail. The lawn kept short. The clothes in the cupboards, pressed, steamed. Simple nutritious meals in the freezer. Dust kept at bay. A favourite mug with a crack that lengthens filament by filament.

Art arrives in the kitchen. She sets the small dish of tablets by his plate.

"Morning."

"Morning."

Mentioning the pills invites argument, so she does not. One for the heart. One for blood pressure. One for mood. He lines his knife parallel to the plate, the old neatness intact. Everything always parallel.

After breakfast she borrows his phone. The contacts resemble a coastline of names worn down by weather. Men from the bowls club. Men from teaching. First names that once needed no surnames. She sends small messages. *Coffee later. A walk. Match on TV on Saturday.* Punctuation perfect, no emojis. She writes like a man for men. Replies arrive. She does not chase.

On the fridge, the list is the spine of the day. Items migrate along it the way birds shift on a wire. She writes small with a fine black pen because small makes the list look shorter.

She walks the foreshore while the day still remembers the dark. Two pelicans at the boat ramp. A runner whose dog keeps to his knee. The woman with the long plait appears at the same bend as always and never nods. Regularities. A sentence of graffiti begins and loses its nerve. A large winter moth clings to a Norfolk pine like a dead leaf. Later, when the day pinches, she can think: the pelicans were in place; the oranges at the grocer's were sweet.

She is a small woman in many ways, but inside she is grand. An opera singer with a huge voice, an author with an oeuvre, a person with opinions that matter.

Where is he? The man I once met. Those long conversations. He was the manager of nearly everything. He still dominates the conversation but he's got nothing to say.

When she returns, Art grazes headlines and stacks the paper into a tidy pile. She sets a glass of water at his elbow. He lifts a photograph of a politician with rolled sleeves and gives a small, late smile. The phone buzzes once. Dale. Ten o'clock works.

Art rises to it almost invisibly. He goes to fetch his hat and returns without it. She waits.

"Back door," she finally says. "Second hook."

He nods and leaves again, and this time the hat comes back with him.

The front bed needs weeding where the rosemary has gone feral.

Ruth, the neighbour, calls a greeting and something about the heat and asks if Joy wants anything from the shops.

"No, thanks."

Inside, Art announces the chair with the bad leg will be sorted in the shed this afternoon. He embarks on a lengthy explanation that she doesn't listen to.

"Good," she says, the praise quiet enough not to provoke resistance, audible enough to prevent a slump. Maintenance of tone is crucial.

She puts his shoes near his feet. He pulls his socks up. He feels for the left shoe with his foot. Does not find it. She guides his foot. He feels for the right shoe. Ties his laces. Pulls the socks up again while pointing his chin to the ceiling as if he is in pain.

"Hurts?"

He shakes his head.

Ten o'clock arrives. At the gate, Dale's nod is short. "Breakwater?" he says.

"Breakwater," Art replies.

They set off at a pace that is excruciating. She watches until the curve of the street swallows them. Empty, the house is suddenly full of possibilities. She could write. She makes tea instead, chooses a mug, sits at the table and writes another list; a private one that does not live on the fridge.

Read a chapter.

Move the rosemary cuttings to shade.

Call the library about the large-print order.

Consider the carers' group flyer from the GP's newsletter. "Consider", not "ring". The softer verb gives her head space.

Light moves across the tiles. A delivery van passes. Somewhere a child practises the same bar of a piano piece. She reads carefully, letting her eyes skid past any sentence that threatens romance. She braces at romance. Cannot imagine it was once in her life too. She imagines two mornings a week that belong to her. *To write my second book at last.* Maybe she should title it *The Mankeeper.*

The men return with salt on their sleeves. Dale stays on the path. "Next Wednesday," he says, choosing a day without consulting her.

"Same time," Art answers.

She brings water to the gate and retreats before gratitude turns into fuss. On the calendar she does not ink it in. She writes it on a small square and tucks it under the fish-shaped magnet. Ink announces too loudly. Paper can be removed.

Late afternoon, she waters the front bed and turns the tap off at the mains rather than trusting the nozzle. Art has explained this to her at length. The first bats lift and stitch the sky. She counts until she loses count. In the shed, the rubber mallet meets oak and the sound reassures her. Competence is not entirely extinct yet. She rolls her eyes and her lips form the word *old.*

At dusk she lays out tomorrow's plate, the small dish of tablets, the pen that does not blot. On a scrap at the door she writes *Hat on the peg.* Whether he will see it, whether seeing will become doing, is not something she can guarantee.

Before bed she looks at the two pillows, one more deeply indented than the other. In the bathroom she counts her own tablets and lets them lie unaligned. Not everything needs to be a parade after all. She looks in the mirror before taking them. Her lips form the word *old.*

When the house goes dark it settles by degrees, timber speaking to timber. A dog barks in the distance. Art breathes heavily. Joy practises a sentence in the brighter tone she saves for him. Perhaps you and Dale could take the TV to the breakwater for the match. Fresh air, good reception. No one has a TV like that anymore. She turns the sentences over and over in her head.

Then the opera singer takes over. *We were the perfect couple. He so competent. I second fiddle. We travelled the entire country. Always remote. He is excellent with the Aboriginal people. So was I, but in a more quiet way. No resentment then. Now I want to scream: Where are you! Stop these long explanations!*

Sleep comes, not quickly, but cleanly. A kind of falling. Morning will ask for the work again. She believes she can answer, but why are her cheeks aching so?

The Bowls Club Afternoon

The afternoon is relentlessly hot. At the club whites glare. The green gives back the sun. Joy sits on the low timber bench beneath the shade cloth. She has brought a bottle of water wrapped in a tea towel and a hat with a wide brim.

Art stands with his team in a neat row, shoes shining, jaw set in the old way that once meant competence and now can mean anything. He has just finished explaining something. She had to suppress a scream. Men greet each other in careful increments. Names are used sparingly, nicknames more often. The coachy one with the whistle voice calls out the rink numbers and the afternoon moves to schedule. Joy has her place behind the tidy border of agapanthus. She knows the etiquette. Wives watch. They applaud the right shots and the near misses that deserve to be honoured. They fetch water.

The first ends are calm. Art's arm swings with the memory of accuracy. He nods at a compliment. Joy relaxes her shoulders an inch. She watches his steps on the mat, the small checks he makes with his eyes, the way he still squares the world before he releases anything into it. She notes the small queue at the bar. Lemon cordial. Light beer. In paper cups that collapse if you grip them too hard.

A man from another rink walks past, pauses, says: "Good to see you, mate."

Art turns his head, smiles, says: "You too".

Play resumes. The mat is placed. Bowls cradle the grass. Between ends, a small gaggle forms near the esky. Talk is ordinary. Weather. The funding for a new shade cloth. Someone's knee. Someone's daughter who moved to Perth.

Art stands slightly apart now, near enough to be included, far enough not to be tested. Joy watches his hands. When he is confident, they describe shapes in the air. When he is not, they hold the rim of the esky.

She rises and walks the long way to the amenities block, past the noticeboard. Working bee Saturday. Names of members who have not paid subs yet typed in a small font to preserve dignity. A flyer for the Men's Shed over in the industrial estate with a photograph of four men in high-vis holding mugs. She reads the times and tucks them into her memory. *If only he would get out more. Leave me some room. Not that he's loud. But he's so present.*

On the way back she stops at the counter and asks for two cordials. The volunteer with the sunburned nose mishears and gives her three. She carries them carefully and sets one by Art's chair. He says: "Ta."

She takes the far end of the bench where shade is thin and pretends to study the notice about the mixed pairs competition. "Mixed" has always meant women who will carry the conversation and smile at the right time. The late sun shifts and flattens the green. A measure is taken with the rigid tape and then with the soft string, as if two kinds of precision are better than one. Art is called on to read it. He appears to mishear and steps forward too late. Another man leans in and does it instead, deferentially and friendly. Joy feels the small displacement in her own ribs.

She keeps her face calm. Inside the opera singer sings loudly. *Who are you? Where are you? Old old old.* She feels like pulling faces, like a child.

At afternoon tea the trestle tables in the hall display slices; pink and yellow and brown. Sausage rolls. Tea in urns. Joy stands behind Art and places a plate and then steps sideways so he can appear to have chosen it. A woman she vaguely knows says, "You two are such stalwarts."

Joy says: "It's good to get him out."

The woman nods.

A raffle is announced. A meat tray. A voucher for the nursery. Numbers are pulled with drama. Art holds his ticket. He does not win. On the way back to the green he catches at her sleeve very lightly, the way a child might. The touch is not pleading. It is a calibration, as if checking he is still moving on the same plane as she is.

The last ends look like the first but feel longer. A wind comes across from the creek and lifts the collars of shirts; it is as if the men have butterflies under their chins. Shadows stretch. A young man from another club, visiting, sends down a bowl with more ambition than sense and the older men smile. Art has one more good delivery in him. It settles where it should and is admired. He had a teacher's sense of restraint once and some of it remains. When it is over, people say: Good game. Hot one. See you next time. On the gravel by the car, Art pats his pockets in search of keys that are in his hand. Joy looks at the horizon while he discovers them. She does not interfere. He unlocks the door. In the passenger seat she places the hat brim up on the back seat the way he prefers. They drive home the slow way along the water, where the tide has finished going out and begun to come back in.

Art says: "Good bloke, that fellow on rink five."

"Yes."

"We should have them over sometime."

"Let's wait and see."

At home she shakes his shirt out over the back step and hangs it where the air will find it. He goes to the shed and stands, not quite entering. She rinses the water bottle and folds the tea towel and writes on the fridge list: *ask about mixed pairs dates, look up nursery voucher for Ruth, polish shoes before Saturday.* She allows herself one thick line through an item already ~~done~~.

In the evening, they sit side by side with the news. The presenter has perfect posture and eyebrows that move. Somewhere there has been a storm. Somewhere a child has done something worthy. Somewhere a politician has rolled up his sleeves. Art says, "I could hear the creek today."

"Yes."

"It smelled of grass."

"They've cut it very short."

He nods.

Before bed she takes his phone and enters *Dale, Wednesday, 2 pm* beneath a previous note that reads ~~dentist~~. She leaves the screen open and props it against the jug so he will have to move it to pour water. She lays out the small dish of tablets and the white plate he prefers and the pen that does not blot. On a scrap she writes *Breakwater, if not too windy.*

In the dark, the day simplifies. She's done the laundry and the shopping. The lapse at the club is like a pebble in a shoe. You can walk with it. It will not kill you. But you will be aware of it with each step until you stop and take it out. She closes her eyes and tries out a new sentence in the brighter voice she saves for him. *How about pairs this year, if Dale is keen. Fresh air.* The words feel serviceable. Morning will test them.

She is enormous. She fills the entire house, neighbourhood, town, beyond. Then why is she allowed no space, no space at all? She must write my next book. Before she die sor he does. Where is he? Does she still love him at all? Sleep comes suddenly. Like falling.

3

Household Barometers

Morning begins with the small audit she no longer names. The kettle, the clock, the calendar, the plants on the sill. She checks the cool bag in the freezer where she keeps ice bricks for hot days and headaches. She taps the thermometer that hangs beside the back door. The kettle offers the first report. If the boil is brisk, the day can be steered. If it fusses, lid rattling, a small sulk in the element, she allows more time between steps and speaks less. Today it behaves. Steam rises. She warms the lemon mug for him and her one and pours without testing the crack.

Art shaves after breakfast. She listens for the even drone of the electric razor through the bathroom door. A steady note means patience; a fast, annoyed burr means she will find whiskers under his ear and choose not to mention them. Today the sound is measured. He comes out with the towel folded and places it on the rail with ceremony. The neatness relieves her and costs her at once. She moves through the rooms, adjusting things. He wants things a certain way. The calendar over the desk shows last month because the picture pleases him. She leaves it. In the hallway she slows at the console table where the keys live in a bowl. She finds a deeper dish in the back of the cupboard; a blue one they brought home from a market when

Brendan was small and moves the keys into it. It is more visible than the first one.

"Where are my keys?" he will ask.

"Same place," she will say. "Different bowl."

In the laundry the water kicks in, the pipes sound like distant frogs. She measures a palm of powder and tells herself small restraints accumulate the way silt builds a bank. On the bench sits the spray bottle she labelled GLASS. She has begun to label for him. She may as well continue. She prints the word CUTLERY on a strip and fixes it on the second drawer.

In the bedroom she opens the top drawer of his chest and sifts through the socks. Three pairs still rolled tight. Four loose. A single black one with the heel worn to gauze. She discards it without ceremony and moves on to the shirts. She chooses one and hangs it on the wardrobe door. The gesture is a flag planted: we intend to get dressed today; we intend to leave the house.

On the table near the window is the bowl of lemons from Ruth's tree. She lines three on the sill where the light will make them gloss. She writes: *lemon butter?* at the end of the fridge list, then crosses out the question mark. She will make it.

The post arrives mid-morning with its mixture of bills. A glossy folded sheet addresses them as *Dear Homeowner* in a bad font, a letter from the council about a change to bin days and a reminder from the optometrist follow. She holds the reminder between two fingers like a wild specimen. He will fuss about new frames and then forget to put them on. She writes *Optometrist* on the list and tucks the letter under the magnet shaped like a fish with Dale's note, the bin schedule, and a cartoon Ruth slid under the door.

Art attempts the crossword and abandons it. He explains the meaning of the word *onomatopoeia*. She doesn't listen. He aligns the paper sections until they lie flat and perfectly stacked and then pushes the stack away with the edge of his hand, an old teacher's gesture of finished. The gesture means nothing now. He stands and announces the shed. She nods. At the threshold he hesitates. The mallet thuds a minute later, proof of a task he may or may not complete. She forms the word *old* with her lips. She finds herself raising her two hands to her nose and form a long nose into his direction, like a child. She takes the compost out and checks the worm farm. She lifts the lid, and a small cloud of gnats lifts with it, then settles. She makes a note to turn it on Thursday and hears herself sigh at the word *note*.

Ruth's hedge throws a ragged shadow across the path. Ruth herself appears, carrying a jar of apricot jam. "Too hot to think," she says.

"Thinking doesn't help much anyway," Joy says, taking the jar.

"You could come with me Friday. Bingo."

"I'll wait and see." The phrase has become a landing pad she uses for everything.

Ruth nods. "He's all right?"

"In the shed."

Ruth's *good* is a barometer reading. Stable enough for now. When Ruth has gone, the house is quiet. The hall clock ticks, steady, impartial, a metronome. She thinks of Brendan, somewhere between here and a mine site, sending messages at hours that do not belong to this household. He will ask whether they have enough batteries for the torches and whether the smoke alarms are in date. She will say *yes. Batteries can be bought. Alarms beep when they need changing.*

She sits at the desk and opens the small drawer where she keeps stamps, paper clips, a glue stick. She finds a roll of masking tape and writes *Old TV* on it and fixes the strip to the sideboard where the old TV lives. She takes it out, unfolds the antennae, and winds the tuner until a cricket commentary swims into shape and then fades. She winds back to a station that tells the weather for the districts and rests there. The announcer lists towns in an order that has not changed since she was a girl. She lets them pass through her. Then she checks the compartment where the batteries sit. When did they buy this TV? Somewhere in the 1070s?

Art returns briefly to the kitchen, removes the lemon mug from the rack and places it to the left of the sink, as if to mark a claim. He says, "Screws too soft."

"Try the tin by the drill," she says without looking up. He goes back out and the shed door makes its hollow sound. She writes *screws; check sizes* on the small list she keeps in her wallet, the one that travels.

At midday, heat collects in the hallway. She closes the bedroom door to keep it out. Lunch is bread and the last of the cheese and salted tomatoes. He eats with the even chew that drives her crazy and wipes his mouth in a way she detests, folds the serviette, and places it on the plate to signal finished. He embarks on an explanation. She does not listen.

"Good," she says when he's done.

She feels kinder towards him for a second.

After lunch he dozes in a chair. His breath thins and catches like a thread sometimes, then runs true. She tries to suppress a sudden surge of hatred. *Why can't I rest with my mouth wide open?* She suppresses the need to scream.

She checks the power board behind the old TV and finds two cords with slack. She tapes them back like he wants it and replaces the side-table bulb before it fails, because failure requires an apology. She stands in the doorway and inspects the room the way one inspects an auditorium before a performance. As if she is an opera singer about to perform. Again, she wants to scream. It's a physical urge, not a psychological one. It makes her throat and cheeks hurt.

When he wakes, the light has shifted. Everything is itself. He says, "What's the time?" though the clock sits at his elbow.

"Two."

He nods and asks, "Today's Wednesday?"

"Thursday."

He blinks.

She hums.

He seems irritated by her humming.

She stops humming.

In the late afternoon a small storm gathers inland. She can taste it before she sees it. The air fattens, the leaves of Ruth's lemon tree turn a paler green and show their undersides, the way fish do when the river changes its mind. She opens the windows on the sheltered side and moves the washing in. The first drop hits the step and leaves a perfect dark coin. In the shed the mallet stops. Art appears with the chair under his arm, like a man carrying a sleeping child. "Fixed," he says.

"Looks sound." Her praise is correctly calibrated. He sets the chair down and presses on it, testing. It does not wobble. He rocks it anyway, for the pleasure of confirming what he already knows. He explains how he's done it. She doesn't listen.

"Good," she says.

The rain does not commit. It teases the dust and then moves away. The smell it leaves is the smell of a childhood summer. She lets the memory form and then lets it sit. Childhood is soothing. Present is not.

Evening gathers with its usual cutlery, plates, and a small dish of tablets. She writes a neat *2* beside the word *lemons* and a single tick beside *screws* to remind herself she has not forgotten. On the new

TV someone declares that clouds are an old-fashioned way to tell weather. She looks at the western sky and knows they are wrong.

Art explains something about predicting the weather over dinner. She does not listen but says: "Good."

After the meal she wipes the table with the cloth from the oven rail. She leaves the cloth there to dry and resists the urge to refold it for neatness. Not everything needs to be prepared for inspection.

Before bed, one final circuit. Windows on latch. Back door bolted. Keys in the bowl. She leans into the hall and watches the clock hands. She smooths the quilt on the sideboard with the flat of her palm, not because it needs smoothing but because her hand remembers. The house settles by degrees.

In the dark she names tomorrow morning's instruments; kettle, TV, mallet, hat, the pen that does not blot. The ache in her cheeks arrives later. "Weather coming in," she whispers to no one, and the phrase stands in for plan, for hope, for the stubborn belief that barometers exist so that storms can be met.

Social gatherings most important. Then movement. Then brain exercise. My book. I must take notes. My face feels tied. My cheekbones hurt. My throat pushes screams. I'm fading. She pinches her skin in several places. *This is me.* She closes her eyes. Morning will ask again. She will read what the house tells her and answer in kind.

4

Brendan's Call

The phone rings in the late morning when shade is shallow. She lets it reach the second buzz. Brendan's name is a blue strip across the glass. She wipes her hand on a tea towel and takes the call at the kitchen bench where the reception is best.

"Mum."

"Brendan."

"How's the old boy?"

"In the shed." She keeps her voice even. "Chair with the bad leg. He's already repaired it but took it back to the shed for some reason."

"Good. Keeping busy is the ticket." He sounds cheerful. A generator hums behind him, wind through a microphone. "So, I can do Saturday. Arvo. Quick one."

"Saturday." She looks at the fridge list.

"Say twelve-thirty? I'll shoot through. Back by five."

"Twelve-thirty is lunch."

"Perfect. I'll grab something on the way." He doesn't mean it. "Or whatever's easy."

She puts the pen on the bench so it won't click in her hand. "We'll make sandwiches."

"Legend." A pause. "Is he... you know... tracking all right, sort of?"

"Better with plans. A walk helps." She keeps it simple.

"Right. I'll take him round to the green. Or the point. We can talk footy. Keep it light."

"Light is good."

"Great. And, hey, maybe invite Dale? More blokes, less pressure on him to talk. If he starts, I'll tell him to keep it brief."

"Dale's Wednesday." She looks at the magnet shaped like a fish. "But I'll ask."

"Whatever's easiest," he says. "Oh, and can you text me your Wi-Fi again? Last time it didn't stick."

"It's on the card by the phone."

"Snap a pic?"

She takes the card, squares it on the bench, and photographs it. "Sent."

"You're a star." Steel clanks in the background. "How are you, anyway?"

"Fine."

"Sleeping?"

"Enough."

"Good. I've got to run. Saturday then. 'Bout twelve-thirty. If I'm late, traffic."

"I'll keep it flexible."

"Love you, Mum."

"Love you too." She holds the phone for a while longer.

Art appears in the doorway with sawdust on his sleeves, pleased. "Who was that?"

"Brendan. Saturday."

"Lunch?"

"Yes."

He nods. He returns to the shed. The hollow sound of the door.

I am so bloody bored. She stamps her foot, like a child. She writes on the fridge list: *Sat—Brendan 12.30.* Then on the private one: *bread; tomatoes; ham, crisps, ring Dale?* She takes the old TV from under the sideboard, checks the masking tape label, and turns the dial until the weather voice finds her again. *Who still has a TV like this?*

Saturday: change moving up the coast; showers late. If the weather turns, the point is wind. The green burns. The house is safest. She adds to the list: *clear table; find coasters; move rug.*

The morning shrinks. She finishes sweeping the hall and finds herself sweeping again. The broom head knocks the skirting. She stops. *What am I doing?* She stamps her foot like an angry child.

Ruth's gate clicks. Ruth's shoes on gravel. A knuckle on the frame. "I'll only be a second."

"Come in."

Ruth leans. "Brendan?"

"Saturday."

"You want a slice for the boys?"

"Thank you. Yes."

"Apricot or lemon?"

"Lemon."

"Done." Ruth straightens, looks at the clock, and reads the room.

"Only lunch."

"Lunch is never only," Ruth says, and goes.

Joy folds the tea towel and places it on the rail. She takes the lemon mug down and sets it to the left of the sink because that is where Art looks first. She writes another line: *slice, thank Ruth; ice bricks; set chairs.*

At midday the heat takes the corridor again. She closes the bedroom door. Lunch is the same bread, the same salted tomatoes. Art eats with the same even chew. Her urge to scream is strong.

"Brendan on Saturday."

"Good." He wipes his mouth. "He'll bring the kids?"

"They're at sport."

He nods. "We can watch the callers."

"We can."

After lunch he dozes.

This is the worst part of the day. I cannot breathe freely. I feel like running. Running where? Aaaah.

She rings the green. Mixed pairs is next month. Saturday is busy with a visiting team. The point will be crowded if the wind holds. She thanks and makes another small plan: the breakwater, early, and back before the heat sharpens.

She stands at the sink with two glasses and looks at the yard. *The rosemary needs clipping.* For Saturday she will move the outside chairs under the eaves, not the jacaranda; too many stains. She will put the coaster with the map of Tasmania under the glasses. He will begin talking about Tasmania. She knows the story by heart.

The phone pings. A message from Brendan: *Might be closer to 1. Traffic.* She replies: *Fine. Drive safe.* A second ping: *Anything you need me to bring?* She types: *Just yourself.* Deletes. Types: *Milk if you're passing.* Deletes. Types: *Ham.* Sends.

In the afternoon she takes the good cloth out of the drawer and leaves it folded on the table. She has made a centrepiece. She checks the side-table bulb. She moves the rug edge. She opens the windows on the side where the breeze is best.

Art returns, puts the lemon mug down in the same place. "Saturday," he says.

"Saturday."

"Sandwiches?"

"Yes."

"Ham?"

"If he remembers." She keeps her voice neutral and hears in it the long habit of saying yes. Late afternoon, she writes a small card in the same tidy hand. *Brendan: TV; breakwater if cool; shade if not.* The card is a way to tame what can't be tamed. She tucks it under the fish magnet. with Dale's note; *bin days; optometrist.*

Evening rises. Cutlery, plates, the small dish of tablets. On the TV someone explains soccer tactics. Art listens and nods. After the meal he stands at the sink and rinses a glass "He's busy," he says to the window.

"He is."

"He tries."

"He does."

Art embarks on an explanation about soccer tactics. She does not listen.

"Good."

Before bed she puts the ice bricks in the freezer, checks the battery in the small fan, sets the lemon mug to the left of the sink. She writes on a scrap: *Brendan—1?* She sticks it by the door. She turns off the hall light and listens to the house. In the dark she plans. The ache in her cheeks. She waits. "Old," she says into the quiet. Then the thinking starts. *Is this how it ends? How long for?*

She turns to Art and forms the long nose with her two hands. She sticks out her tongue while doing it. Like a child.

Small Talk at Sunday Service

Sunday has its own order. Clothes laid out the night before. Shoes wiped. His dark tie. The envelope for the plate tucked in her bag with a mint and a pen that writes on hymn sheets without tearing them. She steams the shirt she chose days earlier and leaves it on the wardrobe door where he will see it. All other garments are steamed during the week.

The church sits low and square behind a line of gums. Inside, the fans move the heat from one place to another. She steers them to a pew three from the back, aisle side. Close enough to look like belonging. Far enough to leave early if needed. He takes the end seat and guards it with his knee, a habit from school assemblies.

The service is the usual braid. Notices. Hymn. Reading. Another hymn. The minister smooths his stole. Joy lets the words pass through. She counts the breaths when the congregation stands and the breaths when they sit. She passes him the book opened at the right page. He sings the first line low, then stops. That is fine. Listening is a kind of singing too.

At the peace, hands reach from all directions with the careful brightness people save for this bit. "Peace be with you." "And also with you."

He takes each hand, not quite looking at the person attached. She supplies two names in a whisper when a pause threatens.

"Margaret." "Len."

He nods as if he had known all along.

The lay visitor in the blue dress waits after the final hymn. She is brisk without being rude. "We haven't seen you at Saturday's morning tea," she says. "We should fix that."

"Another time," Joy says. "We've got lunch on."

"Or I can pop round," the woman offers. "I'm in your street on Thursdays. Short visit. Nothing formal."

"Kind of you." Joy keeps her voice light. "We're steady."

"Good to hear." She writes something on her pad without looking down. "Sing out if you need anything."

"Of course."

Outside, the garden bed of marigolds is cheerful to the point of offence. People cluster under the awning with paper cups. Someone passes a plate of biscuits. She steers him through the traffic with a touch at the elbow. A man from the committee stops them. "Working bee Saturday. Can you make it, Art?" He is the kind who speaks to men about men's things in front of women.

Art looks at Joy.

"We've got our son that day," she says. "Another time."

"Right you are. We'll save you a broom."

On the path to the car park she shortens their route by a garden bed and pretends it is about shade. At the car he hands her the keys without knowing he has done it. She opens the door and lays the hat on the back seat. He lowers himself carefully. They drive home the slow way past the oval where teenagers are pretending not to be watched. He says, "That hymn. The one with the line about anchors." She supplies a title. He nods.

He embarks on a long explanation about church donations. She does not listen.

"Good."

At home she hangs the shirt to air and checks the collar. She puts the envelope, now empty, back in her bag so she will not forget to re-fill it later. She writes on the fridge list in the same small hand: *phone Len; ask about hedge trimmer; return casserole dish to Margaret.*

Lunch is the same. He eats and folds his serviette "Nice people," he says to the table.

"They are."

"We should have them over."

"Let's wait and see."

In the afternoon heat the house goes quiet. *This is the hard part. Again.* She places a jug of water and a glass on the hall table where he will see it when he passes and think of drinking without being told. She moves two chairs under the eaves and tests the shade. *He is getting too skinny. Not only his mind is fading, his body is too. He used to be stout. A handsome man. Will I ever write anything else again but lists?*

She sets a coaster on each side of the table, the good ones with maps. If he remarks on Tasmania it means he is pleased. He will embark on a story she's heard a hundred times.

Later, she takes the service leaflet from her bag and tears it neatly into the recycling so it will not multiply in drawers. The lay visitor's name is at the bottom in an ugly font. She could ring. She will not. Not yet. She writes *Thursday?* and then rubs it out with her thumb.

Evening gathers itself. Cutlery, plates, the small dish of tablets. He lifts each pill in turn as if the order matters. She braces.

"What's this one?" he asks.

"For your heart."

"And this?"

"For sleeping."

"I sleep fine."

"That's because of the pill."

He takes it. *A small victory.*

After, he stands at the sink and rinses a glass. "Church was good," he says to the window.

"It was."

"Nice to be out."

"It is."

Before bed she takes care of the shoes and the shirt and the envelope in her bag and feels the calm. She smooths the quilt in the hallway with the flat of her palm and leaves the window on latch. The house settles in small clicks and sighs. In the dark she thinks of the day's names silently: Margaret, Len, the woman in blue. Tomorrow will bring its own lists, it's own people. She sits up with a jolt. Turns on the light. Grabs her notebook and writes: *She goes wide, fills the room, the yard, the town. She looks for him.*

6

The Appointment

Monday has a time on it. *Ten fifteen. GP follow-up.* She writes it twice; on the fridge list and on the small card by the door where hats hang. She lines up the tablet dish, the lemon mug, the keys in the bowl. She sets the shirt out. She leaves the shoes by the chair with the good back. Breakfast is orderly. He eats, wipes his mouth, folds the serviette. "Hot already," he says.

"We'll leave at nine forty-five."

He nods.

She packs the folder: scripts; last bloods; a note with questions that will sound brisk and reasonable. She adds a pen that writes. She checks the Medicare card twice. At nine thirty she says, "Ten minutes."

He says, "Right."

At nine forty she finds him in the shed, looking at the chair. "Time."

He stares at his hands, then at the door, and says, "For what?"

She braces. "Doctor."

"I'm fine."

"It's a check."

"I'm busy."

She looks at the chair, already fixed. "Five minutes to wash. Shoes on."

He comes in, washes his hands, dries, sits. She kneels, places one shoe where it can be found. He looks past it. The clock takes two minutes.

"Shoes," she says.

"I'll wear thongs."

"Not for the surgery."

He sighs, a child's sound in an old man's chest. He puts one shoe on, then stops. She waits.

By the time they reach the car, it is ten. She drives the short way. The parking is full except for one tight space she takes on the second try.

In the foyer the air is cold and smells of hand gel. A child coughs. She gives the name, takes the seats near the door.

He says, "How long?"

"Not long."

He watches the news without seeing it. She watches the door. Ten fifteen becomes ten twenty-seven. She feels the minutes stack. She keeps her hands still in her lap.

"Art?" the receptionist calls, bright as a kettle.

They stand. "Dr Malik is running a little behind," she adds. "Won't be long."

"Fine," Joy says.

At ten forty the door opens. "Arthur." Dr Malik smiles. "Come on in." Inside, the room there is a tray for everything. Art takes the large chair. Joy sits at an angle where she can see his face and the doctor's.

"How have we been?" Dr Malik asks.

"Good," Art says.

"Mostly steady," Joy says. She passes over the scripts and the note. "A few wobbles."

"Wobbles," Art repeats.

Blood pressure. Pulse. Light in the eyes. "Any falls?" the doctor asks.

"No," Art says.

"Just the step last month," Joy says. "Almost. No injury."

"Sleep?" the doctor asks.

"Fine," Art says.

"Shall we keep the tablet for now?" the doctor asks.

Art glances at Joy.

"Yes," she says.

Art shrugs. "If you say so."

"I do," Dr Malik says mildly. He types. "How are the walks?"

"Good," Art says.

"Better with plans," Joy says. "Dale comes on Wednesdays."

"Excellent," the doctor says. He looks at Art. "There's a group at the hall. Tools, small repairs. Worth a try."

Art's mouth twists. "Not my thing, really."

"Maybe not," Dr Malik says. "But sometimes the thing changes when you're inside it."

There is a pause. The doctor prints the scripts, slides them across. "Anything else today?"

Joy glances at her note. "He forgets names," she says. "Sometimes."

"Names come and go for all of us," he says. "But if the going grows, we can check." He turns to Art. "Would you be open to a simple test? Just a baseline. Not today."

"Maybe," Art says, which means no.

"Another time," Joy says.

They leave with the papers in a neat clip. In the car he says, "Waste of time."

"It wasn't," she says. "We have the repeats."

"It was," he insists. He looks out of the window. "He thinks I'm old."

"You are old."

He snorts and lets the window down an inch.

At the pharmacy she queues while he sits on the chair by the blood pressure machine and looks at the cuff. The queue moves by small permissions. When it is her turn, the pharmacist looks at the scripts and at her and says, "Two of these are early."

"Holiday," she lies.

The pharmacist nods and bags. She signs, takes, thanks, leaves. He follows.

Back home the cool of the hallway. She takes the folder to the desk, files the new scripts behind the old, crosses ~~GP~~ off the fridge list. She writes *Thursday—collect rest of tablets* under it.

In the kitchen he stands with the lemon mug in his hand.

How much longer of this?

"Lunch?" she asks in a chipper voice that she doesn't recognise.

"Bread and tomato."

"Yes."

He eats with the even chew. *The chewing drives me crazy. Why?* He wipes his mouth and folds the serviette. "Nice bloke," he says to the window.

Who is he talking about?

"He is."

"Busy."

"They all are."

After lunch he dozes with his mouth open. She does what she was behind on. *I've never hated him. Why should I now? Should I sit next to him and nap?* She checks the appointment card again. She puts the Medicare card back in the purse, the purse back in the drawer, the drawer back in its shutness.

In the afternoon heat she moves the chairs under the eaves a fraction to the left where the shade is thicker. She sharpens the kitchen pencil and writes on the private list: *ask Dale re hall group; screws—No. 8 x 30; lemons—two more.* She adds one more line and stares at it: *baseline test—later.*

When he wakes, he says, "Did we go somewhere?"

Really? "Yes."

"Where?"

"Doctor."

"Oh. All good?"

"All good."

He goes to the shed.

Evening collects its items. Cutlery, plates, the small dish of tablets. He lifts each one in turn.

Here we go again.

"What's this?"

"For your heart."

He swallows. "Right."

She writes *Thursday* beside the word *pharmacy* on the fridge list and leaves the pen there, parallel to the edge, the way he likes it. Outside, the heat fades a little. Inside, the house settles by degrees and tells her the day is done.

In bed she expands. Inspiration floods her. *I am sharp. I am fit. Because I exercise and watch what I eat. He doesn't. Never has. And look, this is the result. I could be anything. I am a writer. I have a publisher. I should be doing great things, but I'm not. Why?*

Sleep comes. She surrenders gratefully.

7

The Fall

The change in weather is small. The lemon tree drops leaves that land face up. She writes on the fridge list: *gutters; check back step mat; book flu shots.*

It happens in the time between one task and the next. She is at the sink. He is taking the recycling out because she asked him three times. The back door opens, the hollow sound of it. Then a scuff, a quick breath cut short, and a thud. She is there in three steps. *Here it comes. Things are getting real.* She almost feels relieved. He is on the brick, sideways, one hand under him, the other still holding the flattened milk cartons. The mat has bunched. His hat lies crown-down in the rosemary.

"Don't move," she says, kneeling. "Breathe."

"I'm fine," he says.

Stay down, for heaven's sake. She checks what she can see. Elbow skin grazed. Knee catching at the fabric. No blood that runs. He tries to sit. She sets a hand on his shoulder and keeps him still.

"Turn onto your back," she says. "Slowly."

He obeys because the voice is one he knows from a long time ago. He stares at the sky.

"Pain?"

"Just my pride," he says, and winces. "Knee."

She brings the chair from the laundry and angles it as a prop. "On three," she says.

He gets himself up on all fours, then with both hands on the chair and a grunt. He sits. The colour has drained from his face.

"Dizzy?"

"A bit."

"Sit."

He sits on the chair while she goes inside for the ice bricks and a clean tea towels. She wraps the knee, the elbow, checks his hands again. "Head?"

"Didn't hit it."

"Good." She logs the time on the private card. *Fall. Ten twenty-three.* She adds: *back step mat—replace.* Then she phones the clinic.

"Slot at eleven twenty if you can make it," the receptionist says.

"We'll make it."

He tries to stand. She lets him with the chair close by. He says, "Bloody mat."

She rolls the mat and leans it against the bin.

In the car he holds the ice to his knee, then to his elbow and watches the houses go by. She says not what she wants to say. Inside of her it screams: *I told you so. You don't look after yourself, you get this.* At the clinic they give their name. They say it simultaneously. The foyer smells of gel. A child coughs. The television shows the weather forecast. When they are called, Dr Malik looks at the knee, the elbow, the hand. He bends the leg a little.

"Just a knock," he says. "No swelling worth worrying about. Ice today. Rest."

Art nods and smiles as if he has been complimented.

Dr Malik glances at Joy. "You all right?"

"I'm fine."

His look says he has heard that before. "Any dizziness?"

"No, " Art says.

Malik writes something and hands over a sheet that repeats what he has just said. "I'll book you for a quick nurse check next week."

Art says, "No need."

"Humour me," the doctor says, mild as ever.

The nurse wraps the gauze with competent hands. "Lucky," she says. "Could've been much worse."

Back home Joy gets him settled in the chair with the good back. Pillow under the knee. Fresh water. The lemon mug to the left of the sink. He dozes with the ice in place and the tea towels over the gauze. She is furious but doesn't show it. She sweeps the bricks. She looks at the step in a new way: height, edge, the place where feet guess wrong. She writes on the private card: *tape edge; non-slip; ask Brendan to drill strip.*

Ruth's gate clicks. "Saw the car gone. Is he all right?"

"A fall. His knee and elbow."

"Bugger." Ruth passes over a loaf. "Bread."

"Thank you."

"Need anything else?"

"We're covered."

"Call if that changes." Ruth looks past her at the cleared step.

Inside, the day narrows. She moves the side table an inch closer to his chair so he won't overreach. She puts the TV remote where his hand falls. She opens the windows on the side that doesn't draft. She places the ice bricks back in the freezer and sets two new ones by his side.

He wakes from his micro nap, frowns at his knee. "When's Brendan?"

"Saturday."

"He'll make a fuss."

"I'll tell him not to."

Lunch is bread from Ruth and cheese and the better tomatoes. He eats with the same even chew. *God help me!* He puts the serviette on the plate as if the ritual might repair the morning. "Sorry," he says, not quite to her.

"It happens."

"Stupid."

"Just a mat." *Why am I not telling him the truth: I told you so! Told you so many times.*

He accepts this. He sleeps again. She screams inside. Her throat hurts.

She phones the hardware store and asks about non-slip. "Aluminium strip with teeth," the voice says. "Comes with screws." She writes: *strip x 2; screws to match.* She adds: *drill battery.*

In the afternoon she makes a quick run, five minutes there, five back. She leaves a note on the bench in case he wakes: *Back in ten.* She throws down the pen with venom. *God help me!* She throws the pen again. The plastic splits. She takes it to the bin on her way to the car. She throws it in the bin hard. She stamps her foot like a child.

The shop smells of fertiliser and oil. The man at the counter wraps the strips in brown paper as if they are fish.

Back home she puts the bag on the table. He is still asleep. His mouth is open. She looks at him for a long time. She edits the fridge list.

The phone rings. The clinic. "Nurse check Tuesday at nine forty." She stands with the receiver under her chin and a new pen in her hand. "We'll be there." She adjusts the fridge list again.

"Where's that blue pen?" He asks.

"What blue pen?"

"It was here this morning."

"I don't know."

A slow shower before evening. *I'm bathing him now.* She puts the plastic stool in the cubicle and lays the towel over it so it will not startle him. She tells him the order. "Elbow first. Then the knee. No heroics." He does as he is told and comes out clean.

Evening collects itself. Cutlery, plates, the small dish of tablets. *Here we go.* He lifts each pill in turn.

"What's this?"

"For your heart."

"And this?"

"For sleeping."

"I sleep fine."

"That's because of the pill."

He nods and takes it. After, he sits with the strip of brown paper on his knee, stroking it with one finger as if it were a pet. "You'll put this down?"

"Tomorrow. When it's cool."

Before bed she tapes the edge of the step as a temporary measure. She tests it with her own foot. She stands in the doorway and feels a rise at her throat. She swallows.

In the dark he says: "Scared you."

"A bit."

"Sorry."

She listens to the house settle, to his breath return to its even run. She rehearses the order for morning: kettle; pills; call Brendan—say nothing extra; fit strip.

She expands. She can be anything. She is sharp. She is fit. She has a thousand ideas. She pictures a book launch in the local bookstore. A lot of audience. She reads, then signs. She closes her eyes. Autumn has arrived. The work is the same work, but the edges are sharper maybe. She believes she can meet them. *How long for?*

8

A Calendar Blooms

Tuesday she brings the strip and drill to the back step, measures twice, screws once, twice, four times. Teeth bite the brick. Done. He tests it with the edge of his shoe and it satisfied. One risk down. Others queue. She can handle them. She does not need Brendan to things on his day off.

She takes the kitchen calendar down and starts putting scaffolding under the week. *Nurse check. Pharmacy pickup. Dale, Wednesday two. Short walk Thursday morning. Friday: quick trim of the hedge with Ruth. Saturday: Brendan. Sunday: service; leave early.* She writes small to fit it all. The month looks busy enough. *Busy with nothing.*

Calls next. She rings the club and asks about the mixed pairs dates, not because she wants to enter but because dates look like purpose. She rings the community centre. A woman called Mara answers on the second ring.

"Men's morning is Tuesday," Mara says. "Tools, small repairs."

"He has Wednesdays with a mate."

"Nothing wrong with two anchors," Mara says. "You can try it and not come back if it doesn't work."

"I'll think about it."

"Bring him or don't. Your call."

Joy makes three more calls on his phone. Dale to confirm Wednesday. Len to float Friday's hedge. Brendan to say *ten minutes early helps*. Two pick up. One doesn't. She leaves messages that sound like a man does: time, place, nothing extra.

Mid-morning she walks him to the corner and back. He sets the pace. It is slower than ever. A neighbour drives by and brakes. Window down. "How's the knee?"

How does he know? She smiles.

Art says: "All good," and lifts the leg two centimetres to prove it. The neighbour gives a thumbs up and goes.

Back home she slots in a GP follow-up for herself. Not urgent. A referral. A notch on the calendar. She calls her book group and leaves a message on the coordinator's voicemail. "Apologies for Thursday. Family." She doesn't bother with the detail that will only invite interest.

Wednesday, Dale arrives on time.

"Breakwater?" Art says before the knock is finished. Joy steps back.

They go, the slow straight way.

She sets an alarm for three in case weather or chat or pride runs over. While they're gone she reads the three pages she's working on. It's been months. The first paragraph is a list of nouns. The second loses patience. The third admits defeat. She deletes all three and reshapes the morning around errands: *chemist, post, milk*. When the alarm buzzes, she is home with bags and an odd lightness.

They return smelling of salt. Dale says: "Next week," and leaves it hanging for Art to claim. Art claims it. "Two o'clock," he says, and in that small sentence is the day's lift.

Thursday, the nurse check. Weight, wound, pulse. The numbers sit where they should. "Keep walking," the nurse says. "Not heroic distances." They nod.

On the way home she detours past the hall where the men's morning meets. Outside, three blokes in old shirts are arguing amiably about how to sharpen a hoe. Inside, a radio mutters commentary that fills gaps. Art says, "Next time," which could mean anything.

At home she draws a tidy grid on a sheet of paper and writes times in boxes. *Breakfast. Walk. Shed. Rest. Calls.* She puts it on the fridge beside the calendar. When he spots it, he says nothing, only points to Wednesday and nods at Dale's name. He then taps it twice. This tapping is new. It drives her crazy.

Why tap everything? We used to travel the Outback. Work with the Aborigines. You were good at it. Where is that man?

By Friday the week feels overfull. She rings Len. "Ten tomorrow for the hedge on the far side?" Len says yes, arrives at nine forty with a trimmer and a yarn about a pothole. Art stands with them, hands in pockets, offering the old teacher's commentary—"watch your lead," "mind the cable"—and looks steadier for having been needed.

Brendan texts: *Might be one-thirty.* Then: *Traffic.* Then: *Closer to two.* She replies with single words. *Fine. Noted.* He sends a thumbs up, then asks if he should bring anything. She types *No.* Sends it. Deletes the follow-up she nearly added (*just yourself*) and lets the short reply stand.

She catches herself building more supports. She writes out a short list for Sunday—names they're likely to meet, the hymn that has the word "anchors", the lane to the side door if they need the quick exit—and folds it into the back of her purse. She tapes the rug edge by the hallway even though no-one has tripped on it. She moves the chairs under the eaves a second time, chasing a patch of shade that keeps moving.

In the early evening Ruth knocks and hands over the promised slice in a tin with a lid. "For the boys," she says, and then, lower, "How's your face?"

"What about it?"

"You grind your teeth when you're doing other people's thinking," Ruth says. "You were doing it on Tuesday."

"I'll stop," Joy says and touches her cheeks. Her lips form the word *old*.

Ruth laughs.

Saturday morning, everything is staged without looking staged. Plates out. Coasters out. The good cloth still folded. He asks: "What time?" twice in an hour.

"Soon," she says both times, and marks a neat line through one more task on the private sheet: ~~wipe back step.~~

He tries the chair he fixed, sits, waits. "Dale Wednesday?" he asks.

"Yes."

"Men's thing Tuesday?"

"Maybe. We'll see"

He grunts, neutral, which is progress.

Just past two, Brendan arrives. Ute, dust, sun-glare, the sound of a door. He hugs her with one arm while fishing in his pocket with the other. He hugs his father with the same arm and a quick pat. "How's the knee, the elbow?" he asks.

"Fine," Art says. He taps his thigh with two fingers as if he's checking a plank for hollows. Then his arm.

The tapping. God help me.

They eat simple. Brendan has not brought ham. He talks work, kids, a mate's boat. He says: "we should do the point one day." When he rises, it is to the sink. He rinses a glass and leaves it to drain, almost parallel, like his father likes it, not quite.

"Walk?" Joy prompts lightly.

Brendan looks at the clock, then at his phone. "Maybe just a lap to the corner."

They go. She watches them from the doorway. The pace is not equal. On the way back Brendan points at the step strip and says, "Smart."

Art says, "Your mother."

She suddenly remembers who she once was. Attractive. Strong willed. Her own person. Beside him. Not his mother. *I've never asked for this.* She feels fury claim her body.

In the late afternoon, Brendan checks his watch and hugs them both again. "Next week?" he says, making it sound like a plan he might keep. "Text me."

"Will do," she says. She won't. *Two manchildren.*

When the ute goes, the house exhales. She clears the plates with economy and leaves the tin with the slice on the bench, lid ajar, so it looks like an invitation. He sits. He says, "Good visit."

"Yes," she says in the voice she doesn't recognise.

By evening the calendar has new ink. ~~Nurse check done. Len done. Brendan done.~~ Dale holds his square. She looks at the grid and knows she has turned a week into a structure that can hold some weight. It won't hold all of it. Nothing does. But the page looks sturdy, which is something.

She puts the new pen down hard. Tomorrow can sit without a line under it. He turns off the light in the kitchen when she's still sitting there. *It has come to this.* She sits with her face in her hands for a while. *How can I sleep in the same room?*

She lies at the far edge of the bed feeling strangely expanded. Hope surges through her. It's a free-floating hope, not directed at anything.

9

Ruth and the Hedge

Monday is cooler. She brings out the trimmer and the extension lead. The hedge at Ruth's side has gone soft on top and ragged on the sides. Ruth appears with secateurs and a hat that means business.

"I'll do the path side," Ruth says. "You take the inside."

"Deal."

They work without commentary. Cut, lift, bin. The smell is clean and sharp. A car passes, slows, goes on. A magpie watches from the power line.

Ruth breaks first. "How'd Saturday go?"

"Fine," Joy says. "He came. He walked to the corner. We had your slices. No ham. He left."

"On time?"

"Later."

Ruth clips a stubborn twig and lets it fall. "You're grinding your teeth again."

"Am I." Joy keeps cutting. The lead catches on the gate and gives a tug. She frees it. "He's all right with a plan," she says. "Not good without one. He's started tapping things."

"Most men aren't." Ruth leans back, squints along the top of the hedge, trims a small island. "Tapping things?"

"As if to remind himself. He even taps himself." Joy empties the green bin and comes back with two hands free. "I don't want to be unkind," she says.

"Kindness isn't the same as doing everything," Ruth says. "People confuse them."

"I'm going to a counsellor."

"How's that?"

"Haven't been yet. Next week's the first time. Don't say anything."

"Okay."

They swap sides. The thin rain from last night has made the leaves compliant. Art opens the shed door, looks out, closes it again. She knows the sound without looking.

"You going to that Tuesday thing?" Ruth asks. "The tools thing."

"Maybe. We'll see."

"Go," Ruth says. "Let him say no to someone else for a change. Explain things there."

Joy laughs, short.

"And if he says yes, you get two hours without looking over your shoulder."

Joy trims the corner near the step strip and checks the screws. Solid. "I made a grid," she says. "Times. Boxes."

Ruth's mouth twitches.

"It helps."

"It also locks," Ruth says, not unkind.

They stop for water. Ruth leans on the low wall. "Ken wouldn't go to anything with a name," she says. "Men's Breakfast, Men's Shed, Men's Group. Thought he'd be recruited."

"By who?"

"Anyone," Ruth says. "He came round in the last year. Quietly. Too late, but I appreciated the gesture."

"How did you not carry him?" Joy asks. The question is out before she decides to ask it.

"I did," Ruth says. "Then I put some of it down." She ticks items off on the air with the secateurs. "I stopped booking other people. I left his phone where he left it. I let him miss a morning tea and come home cross with himself."

"That sounds hard."

"It was easier than being cross for him," Ruth says. "And people started noticing him again. Funny, that."

They go back to work. The hedge takes shape: flat top, neat sides, a clean reveal of fence and gate. Joy sweeps the path in slow, long pulls.

Ruth says, "Your'e writing?"

"A little."

"Good."

"It's not good," Joy says. "But it's something. Mainly notes."

"That's what good looks like at our age," Ruth says. "Something."

They carry the last armfuls to the bin. The trimmer goes away clean, cord loosely coiled. The job is done. Ruth takes off her hat, shakes out her hair. "Right. Tea."

They sit at Joy's kitchen table with two mugs and a plate of the lemon slice Ruth brought on Saturday.

"You're thin in the face," Ruth says, matter-of-factly.

"I'm eating," Joy says.

"Eat more," Ruth says. "And put him in front of other men for at least two hours a week that you didn't arrange."

"I arrange Dale."

"Then stop arranging Dale," Ruth says. "Let Dale knock and be missed if he's missed."

Joy turns the mug once. "I know what to do," she says. "Doing it is the trick."

Ruth stands, rinses her cup, dries it with the tea towel on the rail. "I'll ring the hall and tell Mara you will come," she says. "You can ignore it if you like."

"Don't," Joy says.

"Tuesday, then. I'll walk you as far as the door if that helps."

"It doesn't."

"Better," Ruth says. At the door she taps the edge of the step strip with her shoe. "Smart. Put another on the front. Just in case."

"My whole life is one big just in case."

"I know."

When Ruth has gone, the house feels level. Joy stands at the window and looks at the hedge and decides not to cross it off any list.

Art comes in from the shed. "Looks good," he says, meaning the hedge.

"Ruth," she says.

"Tell her thanks," he says. He reaches for the lemon mug, sets it to the left of the sink and turns. "Tuesday?" he asks, surprising her.

"Men's morning," she says. "You don't have to."

"Tools."

"Tools."

He nods once. "We'll wait and see."

"I'm going to write for an hour," she says. "Door open."

"Right," he says. He doesn't follow. She makes a little jump. Like a child.

She goes to the small room and puts the chair where the light works. She sets a timer for sixty minutes and starts with one paragraph. No metaphors. No weather. Just the scene at the bowls club with the name that didn't arrive and the way the pause felt like someone putting a hand on the back of her neck. She writes it. It holds. When the timer goes, she stops. She doesn't fix it. She leaves the file open and the chair pushed in and the pencil where it lies. She does not reward herself and she does not scold herself. She checks the calendar: *Tuesday—Hall, 10. Wednesday—Dale, 2. ~~Thursday—Nurse, 9.40 (done). Saturday—Brendan (done).~~* She draws a small line under Tuesday.

In the late afternoon she and Art take the slow walk to the corner and back. He points at the repaired chair through the shed window. "Good job," he says.

"It is," she says.

He goes into the shed to fetch the chair and put it in the living room for the third time.

At dinner there is no talk about pills or sleep. Has her face said enough? He eats, folds the serviette, stands. "I'll be right for Tuesday," he says.

"Okay," she says.

"Ten?"

"Ten."

He nods. He rinses his glass and leaves it to dry. It stands almost parallel to the edge of the sink.

Before bed she puts the small card by the door: *Hall—10.* She turns out the light and expands. She is wearing fantastic clothes. A gown. Red high heels. She is a diva. Yes, that what she is. Until sleep claims her.

The Men's Morning

Tuesday. Hall at ten. She writes nothing else. She sticks it to the bathroom mirror.

They walk the two blocks. He carries nothing. She brings a small card with his name and number and puts it in his pocket. The hall doors are propped with two paint tins. Inside: trestles, a bench, a tub of mixed screws, tools, three men already there. One waves them in without ceremony.

"Mara," the woman says, coming from the office. "You must be Art." She shakes his hand. "Kettle's on. Jobs are small. For the op shop. Stay as long as you like."

He nods. "Right."

"Two hours," Joy says.

Dale appears five minutes later, surprised but not making a shape of it. "You found it," he says.

"Close enough to walk," Art replies.

Joy stands to the side. She does not hover. She remembers when she dropped off Brendan at preschool for the first time. This feels the same. Mara glances at her. "We've a carers' table at the back if you want to sit," she says. "You can also leave."

"I'll leave," Joy says. "Be back at twelve."

Mara nods. "She turns to the men. "Today we've got a box of loose handles from the op shop and half a dozen garden shears that stick. Oil and cloths are in the crate. Test before you hand back."

Joy hoovers.

Work starts. Someone sorts screws by length. Someone wipes down the trestle. Dale sets a handle in a vice and shows Art the bolt he'll need. Art looks, then looks again, then reaches for the spanner without being told. The old movements are still there.

Joy turns toward the street and walks to the bakery two doors down. She orders a long black and sits by the window with her note-book. She breaths deeply and turns her face to the sky. She writes three lines and stops. She watches the street: one van, one pram with running mum, the florist hosing the pavement. At eleven forty-five she goes back. From the hall door she sees them at the bench. Art holds the shears while Dale oils the hinge. A third man—Ed, accord-ing to his name badge—tests a toaster by plugging it into a board with a big red switch. Mara moves past with a crate of rags. "He's fine," she says quietly to Joy.

"I'll wait."

At twelve, Mara claps once. "Pack up."

The men tidy. Rags in the tub. Oil closed. Tools counted back. Art wipes the bench with the flat of his palm, then with a cloth.

"Next Tuesday," Mara says. "Same time."

Ed nods. Dale nods. Art looks at Joy, then at the bench, then at Mara. "I'll check," he says.

"That's the spirit," Mara says.

Outside, on the path, Joy asks, "How was it?"

"Tools are blunt," he says. A beat. "Good blokes."

"Go again?"

"Maybe. We'll see."

"You're still wearing your name tag."

He looks down and laughs. She laughs too. It's almost like, what? Ten years ago? Fifteen? When they still laughed together about nothing. They walk home the short way. She does not hurry. At the corner he points at a loose paling in the fence and says, "Needs a brace." She keeps her face still.

Back at the house he puts the lemon mug to the left of the sink. "Eleven's enough," he says.

"Good." She does not ask what he means.

He sits in the chair he fixed, checks the leg, and rests. She writes on the calendar: *Hall — maybe.*

Before bed, he turns off the light in the living room while she's still in it. She walks up the stairs in the dark. She's expanded even before her body hits the mattress. She feels like spreading her arms, as if receiving applause. She pictures herself in the glittering black dress, the red high heels. Her legs have always been her best feature. She lifts a pale leg and looks at it.

"What are you doing?" he asks.

"Nothing."

The Family Lunch

Sunday. Brendan again. He said *proper lunch this time.* After church, she quickly put plates out. No tablecloth. No centrepiece. Sandwich fixings in the fridge. A knife on the board. If he wants more, he can ask. He arrives at twelve-forty-five. No kids. Dust on the ute. A bag of rolls in one hand, already crushed. No ham.

"Starving," he says, stepping in. "What've we got?"

"Ham. Tomato. Cheese."

"Nice." He looks around. "Shit! I forgot the ham."

"I know you would."

You didn't—ah—set the table?"

"It's set."

"Oh." He seems confused.

Art comes in from the shed, wipes his hands on a rag, drops the rag in the laundry basket without looking. "G'day."

"G'day, Dad." Brendan claps him on the shoulder. "How's the knee, the elbow?"

"Fine."

They stand at the bench. Joy slices. Brendan opens the rolls and shakes crumbs onto the board. Art pours water. No one takes a plate.

"So," Brendan says, mouth already full. "I was thinking we should do a roast next time. Make a day of it."

"Roast is work," Joy says.

"I can carve," he says, as if that solves it.

She slides a plate from the table across the bench toward him. They eat standing. Brendan talks work. He checks his phone. He puts it face down on the counter and picks it up a minute later.

"Let's plan something big," he says. "Invite Dale. Get the boys over when sport settles. Give Dad something to look forward to."

Art says, "I'm not a project."

Brendan grins.

Art looks at Joy. "Your mother loves structure," he says. "Lists and that." He means it as a joke. It lands wrong. She says nothing. She does not smooth it. She lets it be awkward. She makes her own sandwich and sits at the table. The men stay standing. She does not ask them to sit.

Brendan glances at the empty chairs. "We could—ah—sit?"

"You can," she says. She doesn't move.

He sits. Art sits. The scrape of chairs is louder than the talk. She does not rescue. Brendan tries again. "You doing the club, Dad?"

"When it suits," Art says.

"Keep the brain ticking."

Art's jaw tightens. "It's bowls, Bren. Not a test."

"Right." Brendan clears his throat. "And the men's thing? Tools?"

"Maybe, we'll see," Art says. "The tool are blunt."

Brendan looks at Joy. "What do *you* think, Mum?"

"It's up to him," she says.

Silence. Chew, swallow, drink. Brendan pushes his plate away. "Hey, you know what'd be great? If we pencilled a day each week for me to take him. Saturdays. I'll swing by. Give you a break."

"Don't pencil it," she says. "Just come."

"Work's variable."

"Then don't promise," she says.

He raises both hands. "Fair."

Art frowns. "We're fine," he says. "Your mother fusses."

Joy stills. She looks at him, then at Brendan. "I'm not fussing," she says. "I'm doing. Always doing."

Brendan looks down. "She is, Dad."

Art shrugs. "It's just lunch."

"Exactly," she says, and stands. She leaves the knife where it is and the crumbs on the board. She does not fetch napkins. She does not refill glasses.

Brendan watches her not doing the next thing. "You right, Mum?"

"I'm having my sandwich," she says. "That's all."

He nods. They finish. No tea. No slice. She closes the fridge. Art looks at the closed door.

Brendan clears his plate, hesitates at the sink, then washes it. He washes the knife. He dries both with the tea towel and puts them down. "I'll head off," he says. "Work tomorrow."

"Drive safe," she says.

He hugs them quick. At the door he turns back. "I'll text about next week."

"Don't," she says. "Just come."

He nods and goes. The ute coughs, catches, leaves.

Art stands where he is. "He means well," he says.

"He does."

"He's busy."

"I know."

He looks at the board, the crumbs, the knife, the roll bag. He reaches for the tea towel. She doesn't hand it to him. He finds it himself. He wipes. He rinses the board and leaves it to drain. He puts the knife point down.

"Next time," he says, "just sandwiches again."

"Yes," she says.

He looks at her. "I didn't mean fuss."

"I know what you meant."

She writes nothing on the calendar. She takes nothing off. She sits for ten minutes at the table and does not fill the silence. Then she moves the bin bag out and ties it. The knot holds. That is enough for the hour. She throws the bag in the bin hard and glances at the door. Has he seen that? She kicks the bin.

In bed, her thoughts skip from one image to another. The way they used to be together. *Natural. At ease.* The way she saw herself: a diva. The way she sees him now. The way he sees her.

"You're breathing loud," he says.

"Sorry."

She practices block breathing silently. It helps the expansion come on. She makes the long nose at him and sticks out her tongue.

12

Aftershock

The house is ordinary. Plates are clean. Board drying. Nothing to tidy or clean that would replace thinking. Thinking is driving her crazy. She takes the small card from the drawer and writes a new heading: *Not mine to do.* The first lines come quickly.

Organise Brendan's Saturdays or Sundays
Ring Dale for him
Remind club about him
Fill silences he makes
Find names he forgets
Listen when he says: "yes but."

She stops. Adds one more:

Explain myself

She slides the card under the fish magnet. Leaves it visible.

He reads the paper without turning a page. "Match on later?" he says.

"If you like."

"Dale Wednesday?"

"Up to you."

He looks at the calendar, finds his square. Taps it with his finger twice.

"I'm going to write for one hour. Door closed."

She goes to the small room and opens her file. Yesterday's paragraph is there. She reads it once. She types six plain lines about lunch—*standing, sitting, crumbs*—and saves. She does not push for more. Her psyche does not want to reveal. If that is the case, so be it.

A text from Brendan: *Sorry if I put my foot in it. Will try for next Sat.*

She writes back: *Understood. No need to promise.*

He thumbs-up reacts. She does not reply to the reaction. She used to react to a thumbs-up with a thumbs-up, but she's decides to stop that. It's one less thing to do.

Ruth knocks once and steps in with the ease. "How'd it go?"

"Fine," Joy says.

Ruth tilts her head. "Meaning?"

"He ate. He suggested plans. I didn't accept the job."

Ruth says: "You look less... tight."

Joy moves a shoulder. "We'll see how long it lasts."

"You going Tuesday? Tools?"

"Maybe. We'll see."

Ruth points her chin at the card on the fridge. Reads the heading. Smiles. "Keep that one."

After Ruth goes, Joy makes two calls. The first is to the community centre. "I'll bring him Tuesday."

"Great," Mara says. "He can leave when he wants."

The second is to the bowls club. "We'll skip mixed pairs this month," she tells the volunteer. "If anyone asks, tell them we're steady." She deletes ~~mixed pairs—call~~ from the fridge list.

She sits with a glass of water and lets ten minutes pass without a women's work attached. The glass sweats and makes a circle on the table. She does not wipe.

Late afternoon, she and Art walk to the corner. He sets the pace. He still limps a bit. A neighbour calls from a driveway, "See you Friday for the hedge?"

She says "Yes" without looking at him to check.

Back home, he stands by the bench. "You were sharp today," he says.

"I was clear."

"I can ask Dale myself."

"Yes."

"I can ring the club."

"If you want to."

He looks at the phone. "Maybe tomorrow."

"Tomorrow is fine."

She writes nothing down. She moves nothing to a list.

The evening is simple. She cooks, they eat, he rinses his plate without prompting. He places it in the rack at an angle that would once have bothered him. She leaves it.

Before bed she takes the card from the fridge and copies the heading onto a clean page in her notebook. She does not rewrite the lines. The heading is enough. One less thing to do. She closes the notebook and puts it in the drawer that does not stick.

In the dark, she doesn't rehearse. She lets the day idle to a stop. She expands while block breathing. Her bosom heaves as if after a long and intense song. She opens one arm, because two would make him notice. She is enormous. A phenomenon. An artist. She feels an enormous drive. When sleep comes, it sweeps her off her feet like a lover.

PART II WINTER

13

Boundary One

She circles Thursday on the calendar and writes two word: *Book group.*

Morning is ordinary. Except she does not pre-cook, pre-label, or pre-load. She puts bread, eggs, and fruit where they always are. Easy to find. She puts the cordless on its base. She places his phone on the bench, screen up. She says, "I'm out at two. Back by five. Or six."

He nods. She does not repeat it. He begins to say something. She does not listen.

"Good."

At one-fifty she showers, dresses, takes her bag. On the way out she touches the back of his shoulder with two fingers. "Call if you need me,"

He says, "Right," eyes on the crossword he may not finish.

She walks to the bus stop. On the bus she does not look at her phone. At the book group café, four women sit with paperbacks face down like small tents. Someone says, "Tea?" Someone else says, "You start."

Joy listens, then speaks when it's her turn. No stories about home. She talks about a paragraph and why it worked. Her voice sounds like itself. At three, her phone vibrates once. A missed call from the landline. She doesn't bolt. She texts: *All well?*

Reply, after a minute: *Toast. Smoke alarm. Sorted.*

She types: *Open a window.*

He sends a thumbs up.

She puts the phone face down and stays in her chair. They finish at four-thirty. Outside, the air has thinned. She has not told him about the counsellor. She goes, sits, talks. Says sentences she does not recognise. They roll from her mouth, over her lips, into the room.

"He's old. I don't recognise him. I'm so angry. He fell. It is his own fault that he falls. He does not look after himself. I do everything...."

She does not tell about the diva inside her, the expansion.

"You're grieving," says the counsellor.

"He's not dead yet."

"You're grieving who he once was."

"Rubbish! I'm angry," she corrects.

"Anger is part of the grieving process."

She buys bread on the way to the bus stop and stands without fidgeting. The bus arrives.

Home at six-ten. Would he have noticed the missing hour? Front door unlocked. One kitchen window on latch. A tea towel draped on the deck rail. A slice of toast in the bin, black. He is at the table with the paper set in a neat square and a glass of water half empty.

"Good?" she says.

"Smoke alarm works," he says. A beat. "I opened the window."

"You did."

"Ruth knocked. Said it was loud."

"She would."

"I told her it was toast."

"Good."

He nods. "I made another piece." He points to the plate, crumbs proof.

She puts the bread on the bench and hangs the tea towel on the rail. "Thanks for the text."

"Didn't want you to leave," he says, then corrects himself, "I mean, to have to leave."

"I didn't."

He watches her put the bread away. "Book thing good?"

"Yes."

He waits for more. She gives him one line. "We argued about endings. No one won." That satisfies him.

She checks nothing else. She doesn't look at the smoke alarm. She doesn't ask where the missing matches are. She sits. After dinner he rinses his plate and places it in the rack. Near-enough straight. He says, "Next Thursday, go again."

"I will." *I don't need your permission!*

"Right," he says, settling into the chair he fixed. He taps the arm once, bends forward, taps the leg twice.

Before bed she circles *Book group* on the next Thursday too. She puts the pen down and leaves the calendar alone.

In bed she balances on the far end edge away from him on her side. *Grief. Anger. Am I indeed grieving him? Or am I just angry?* It sits like a ball of hair in her chest. She's like a cat who wants to vomit but cannot. *When will he die? When will I die? What would I do if he does? What would he do if I do?* She imagines his funeral. Heaps of people. She is wearing the black glittering gown and the red high heels. She imagines she takes a rose from his coffin and sticks it in her mouth. Holds it between her lips like a bone. As if she's about to dance the Tango. She dances herself into deep sleep.

14

Boundary Two

Monday. A call from Len: "Cards Thursday at yours?" He says it like last time.

"Not this week," she says. "Try Dale's."

A pause. Len recovers. "Righto. I'll ring him."

She hangs up and does not write anything down.

Art comes in from the shed, sees the phone on the bench. "Len?"

"Yes."

"Thursday?"

"Not here."

He blinks twice. "Why not?"

"I'm out."

He waits for a different answer. None arrives. "We always do second Thursdays."

"Not this one."

He looks at the table. "It's only a few hours."

"Yes."

"Easy."

"Not for me."

He frowns, confused more than angry. "What's hard?"

"Hosting," she says. "Setting up. Making sure you've got what you think arrives by itself."

He laughs. "It's cards."

"It's work," she says. "I'm not doing it this time."

He stands very still. "I didn't ask you to fuss."

"You didn't ask," she says. "That's the point." Silence. He looks older when he is quiet.

"Len'll do it," she adds, softer.

"Right."

Tuesday he moves through rooms and leaves small arrangements out of true. She does not nudge them back. He eats standing. He stands at the sink and leaves the glass skewed. She says nothing.

Wednesday Dale drops by. "Cards at Lenn's?" he says to Art. "Seven."

Art looks at Joy and away. "I'll wait and see," he says.

"Easy transport," Dale adds. "I'll swing by."

Art nods without commitment. Dale shrugs. "No worries," and goes.

That night, over a simple dinner, Art starts small. "You've changed."

"I have," she says.

"You don't have to."

"I do."

He breathes out through his nose. "You've got your groups."

"Two hours a week," she says. "You have Wednesdays with Dale. You can have Thursday without me."

"It's not the same." He pushes his plate back. "They expect the table. The biscuits."

"They can expect elsewhere," she says.

"It's my house," he says.

"It's ours," she says. "And I'm in it."

He closes his eyes. Opens them. "It's just cards," he says again.

She puts her hand flat on the table. "It's been thirty years," she says. "I'm tired."

He stares at her hand, as if it were a new object. "I didn't see," he says. "Sorry."

"I know."

He lifts his shoulders and lets them fall. "All right."

Thursday morning, he doesn't ask. He potters in the shed and comes back with dust on his sleeves. *What has he repaired this time? Nothing's broken.*

At five, the phone rings. Len confirming with Dale confirming with Art. She does not answer. Art does. "Yep," he says. "See you."

At six-thirty he hovers by the door. "Seven," he says, in case she didn't hear.

"Have a good night."

"You're not coming."

"No."

"Right." She helps him with his shoes. He finds his coat. He finds his hat. He checks his pockets, the theatre of departure rehearsed and rusty. At the gate he turns. "Back by nine."

"Enjoy it."

He goes. The night takes him.

She eats on a side plate. She reads a chapter. At eight-thirty she makes tea and drinks it hot without putting a second cup on the bench. She drums on the table with two flat hands. Her hands look old. *Is this what it comes down to then?*

At nine-ten the gate clicks. He comes in with cold on him and the smell of winter.

"How was it?"

"Fine." He unbuttons slowly. "Different."

"Good different?"

He thinks about it. "Enough," he says. Then, after a beat, "They had cheap biscuits."

"Next week take yours," she says. "If you want to."

He looks at her and at her hands that are still flat on the table. "Maybe, we'll see," he says.

He goes to the sink, rinses his clean glass, sets it down almost straight. "Thanks," he says.

"Right," she says.

He stands in the doorway, unsure if the night is finished. "You'll do your group next month?"

"Yes. Every week."

"We'll both be out," he says, as if testing the balance of it.

"We will."

He turns off the kitchen light while she's still in the kitchen. She sits in the dark, shaking her head.

In bed her expansion behaves differently. She becomes large and small. Large and small. At some point she nearly disappears. This causes a jolt of fear; adrenaline. She sits up, hand on her heart.

"What's the matter," he says.

"Nothing," she says.

15

Silence Week

She starts Monday by not sending any messages. No *coffee?* No *walk? No you free?"* She leaves his phone on the bench where he can see it and keeps her hands off it. This is not easy. Morning is plain. Toast. Vegemite. News she doesn't follow. He drifts towards the shed and stops in the doorway. He comes back and straightens the paper he won't read. At ten the phone lights with a scam number. She lets it die. At eleven nothing. At noon, the neighbour reverses poorly and corrects. Ordinary traffic. *When will he move? Do something?*

After lunch he says, "Dale?" He looks at the phone. "Right."

Tuesday she ignores the club notice that pings in the email *pairs postponed due to weather.* She writes nothing on the calendar. She walks to the shop for milk and returns by the longer street. When she comes in he is in the same chair, same angle, the lemon mug in the same position. Fury engulfs her and leaves again like weather.

"Walk?" she offers in the strange voice.

"Cold."

"Later then." *Mistake. Do nothing. No matter what you do. Do nothing. Say nothing.*

Later becomes never. *As usual.* She notes it but does not argue with it. She lets the feelings come and go as the counsellor advised her.

Wednesday would be Dale. She does not text. At one forty-five Art stands by the window, then sits, then stands. At two he says, "He's late."

"He hasn't said he's coming."

"Oh." He sits again.

She makes tea and does not pad it with talk. He drinks it quickly as if he's going out and leaves the cup on the table. She leaves it there.

At four, Dale knocks anyway. "All right for a wander?" he asks.

Art looks at Joy.

"Up to you," she says.

Art hesitates, then says, "Next week." Dale nods. "Ring me," he says to Art, and touches the gate on the way out so it won't swing.

Thursday, Ruth taps once and leans in. "You doing the quiet week?" she asks, eyeing the stillness.

"Yes."

Ruth glances at the phone on the bench. She leaves a bag of lemons. In the afternoon Joy takes the chair with the good back and moves it a hand's width away from the heater.

He notices. "Why?"

"You slouch when it's too warm."

He huffs but doesn't move it back. Ten minutes later he shifts it, annoyed at no one.

She spends an hour with her draft. No scene today. Lists of moments: *the bowl at the club, the pause; Brendan standing instead of sitting; the step strip's neat teeth.* She puts each on its own line and leaves white space between them. It looks like breathing room, which is the real work.

Friday she de-clutters a drawer and finds three old membership cards: library, bowls, RSL. The dates speak. She keeps the library, bins the rest, doesn't ask permission. He is in the shed tapping a nail into wood that doesn't need it.

At lunch he says, "We could call Len."

"You could."

He stares at the phone again. He doesn't touch it. After, he sleeps in the chair, mouth open.

Here we go again. She lets him be ugly. *Love can take it.* She lets the feelings race through her. They leave her exhausted.

The post brings a flyer from the council about a *Men's Wellbeing Expo* with a photo of a man doing a thumbs up. She laughs unseen and drops it in recycling. *The grimmer the world gets the more dumbups. They're everywhere.*

By evening the house seems to have learned the new rule: no prompting. He reaches for whatever he reaches for. He leaves what he leaves. She corrects only what would injure: cord under foot, mat edge, heater dial. The rest she ignores. This is not easy. Her shoulders unknot in tiny clicks she refuses to celebrate.

Saturday, Brendan texts: *Tomorrow? Might swing past.*

She replies: *If you do, you do. No time. No hook.*

He thumbs-up reacts.

She pockets the phone and goes outside to prune the rosemary back hard. He watches her through the window and does not come out to direct. *That's a win.* She takes all her rage out on the pruners and the woody stems.

After lunch she moves the indoor toolbox from the high shelf to the low one. He sees it later and says nothing, just uses it to fix a loose hinge on the freezer. *He understood.* The sound of the screwdriver turning is clean and specific. He stands back, tests the door. "Better," he says to the hinge, not to her. *Sure.*

Sunday morning is spare. Service if they want it.

"Your call," she says.

He says: "Home."

So they are home. She reads because reading is a step toward writing. He half-watches football from last year. When he gets stuck on a name, he doesn't ask. The stuckness passes. Or it doesn't. The day holds anyway. Brendan does not swing past.

Do not promise.

At four, Art goes to the gate and stands there for ten minutes, looking up the street. He returns, quieter, and folds the tea towel with too much precision.

That night he says, "It's quiet."

"It is."

"Too quiet."

"For a week," she says. "It will do."

He nods as if he understands. He turns the glass in his hand and sets it down. "I could ring Dale," he says.

"You could."

"Tomorrow."

"Tomorrow is fine."

He looks at the calendar and at the empty squares where ink should be. "We didn't write," he says.

"We didn't need to."

He takes that in. "I didn't fall."

"No."

"I made toast without burning it."

"Yes."

"I can ring Dale."

"You can."

He nods again. "I'll do it in the morning. Ten." He begins explaining something.

She does not listen.

"Good."

They go to bed early. The week sits behind them like a low fence: stepped over, not impressive, enough to mark a boundary. In the dark she feels the space she won back, small, but real, and does not rush to fill it. She does not want to expand during the daytime, into their real life. She expands when real life seems unbearable. This is what the counsellor said when she told him about it. The counsellor is a funny one. He seems as lonely as she is. When she said something about it, he said that his story is not relevant.

16

Ruth's Kitchen Table

Mid-morning. A tap on the frame and Ruth steps in with her usual economy. "Kettle?" she asks, already halfway to it.

"Please."

"Let's go to your place."

They carry the cups. They sit at Ruth's small table with the two mugs and a plate of Sao biscuits. The hedge through the window holds its line. A wattlebird shouts and moves on.

Ruth waits. Joy breaks a biscuit in half and lines the pieces.

"Silence week," Joy says. "No prompting."

Ruth nods. "And?"

"He didn't fall. He made toast. He stood at the gate and didn't call Brendan."

"Good week," Ruth says.

"It was hard to watch. Hard to do nothing."

"Watching is the tax," Ruth says. "Cheaper than doing it all."

Joy looks at the clean benchtop, the list on Ruth's fridge that has three items. "How did you stop filling the gaps?"

Ruth sips. "I let Ken *feel* them. That was the trick. Not to punish. To show."

"He didn't make you pay for it?"

"Of course he did," Ruth says. "Men call it mood. I called it Tuesday. Then I went for a walk."

Joy smiles. "I told Len to hold cards at his place."

"Progress."

"He went. It was 'different'."

"Different is a start," Ruth says. "Second week he'll sit where someone else tells him. Third week he'll take biscuits."

Joy turns the mug. "I've circled book group again. The counsellor afterwards. Forty-five minutes. He doesn't notice."

"Then go again."

"I will."

Ruth leans back. "You going to the hall tomorrow?"

"He said 'maybe'. I wrote nothing."

Ruth says: "If he goes, you leave. If he doesn't, you still leave for two hours."

"Where?"

"Anywhere," Ruth says. "Sit on the bench near the bakery and do nothing. Count buses."

Joy laughs. "I could write."

"You could sit," Ruth says. "Either counts."

They eat another biscuit each. Ruth flicks a crumb with her nail. "What about Brendan?"

"He texted *tomorrow?* and didn't come."

"Predictable."

"I answered 'if you do, you do'."

"Better."

Joy sits with that. "I keep wanting to stage-manage. It feels like betrayal not to."

"It's refusal," Ruth says. "Betrayal is promising that you can't keep."

They shift to practical things. The step strip on the front. The hedge next month. The light over the sink that flickers. Ruth tops up the mugs. "You talk to the doctor about a baseline?"

"Not yet."

"Put it on paper. Not your fridge. Make him his own file. Let him manage it." Ruth holds Joy's eye. "It's not for him. It's for you."

Joy nods. "I will."

Ruth stands, sits again. "One more thing," she says. "Dale. Stop announcing him."

"I have."

"Then when Dale knocks, don't translate. Let no answer be a no," Ruth says. "He'll miss a walk once and feel the shape of it."

Joy lets the thought settle. "I can do that."

Ruth grins. "You can do anything. That's half your problem."

They walk the mugs back. On the way out she taps the doorjamb with two fingers as if clocking off. "Tea at mine Thursday," she says.

Ruth says: "No talk if you don't want talk."

"Thursday," Joy says. "Thanks."

Back home, Art is at the table with the crossword turned to the easy page. He looks up. "Ruth?"

"Yes."

"She's all right?"

"She is."

"Dale?" he asks, not looking at the phone.

"If you want."

He shrugs. "Maybe, we'll see."

She doesn't rescue him. She sits in the small room with the door closed and opens yesterday's file. She adds three plain lines about the week—*the empty moments, the shape of them, the gate, the hinge on the freezer.* She leaves them unpolished. Truth beats style. She'll do the real work later.

At noon he says, from the doorway, "Tea?"

"Please."

He thinks about this, standing. He brings two mugs. No saucers. The mugs are mismatched but clean. He sets hers on the desk, not on a coaster, and nothing terrible happens. After lunch he goes to the shed and stays. These small silence gives her time and space. She prints the GP's number on a card and puts it in her purse. She writes a line on the private sheet: *Baseline—book.*

Mid-afternoon, Dale knocks. "Walk?"

Art looks at Joy.

Don't look at me. "Up to you," she says.

Art hesitates, then nods. "Right."

"No breakwater," Dale says lightly. "Wind. The oval."

They go. Slow. Twenty minutes later they're back, smelling of wind. At the gate Dale says, "Tuesday at the hall?" to no one in particular.

"Maybe, we'll see" Art says. Dale takes it as a yes, or at least as not a no.

When the house is quiet again, Joy writes one sentence on the page she's building: *He walked without me encouraging.* She doesn't add weight.

Near dusk, Brendan texts: *Friday night? Might swing past after work.*

She types: *If you do, you do.* Sends.

He replies: *Legend.* Then: *Anything to bring?*

She writes: *No.* Leaves it at that.

She defrosts a simple dinner and puts the plate in front of him.

He says, "Thanks." *Not the chewing. So help me God.*

He chews.

Her silent scream rises.

After, he rinses and leaves things where gravity would put them. She leaves them.

Before bed she puts no marks on the calendar. She looks at Tuesday and doesn't underline it. She sets the pen down out of line on purpose then gives it a nasty flick that makes it spin. The house holds its shape without help. She looks around in it while she climbs the stairs. *How long until he can't get up the stairs anymore?*

The expanding comes immediately. She opens her arms to receive the applause. She bows, see her black glittering dress, her red high heels, her good legs in their sparkling stockings. Gratitude, pride, hope, and happiness surge through her.

GP Follow Up

Appointment at nine forty. She writes it on a card and puts it in her pocket, not on the fridge. She can't let him go alone. They arrive on time. Reception is brisk. "Take a seat." The TV is off. A toddler counts chairs. Art reads the sign about masks and does not take one.

"Arthur?" The nurse. Weight. Blood pressure. A pulse clip that leaves a small crescent on his finger. "Steady," she says. "Doctor will be five."

Dr Malik waves them in. "Morning." He looks at Art. "How's the knee holding up?"

"Fine."

"Any stumbles since?"

"No."

He taps the last note. "Sleep?"

"Fine."

"Excellent." He turns the screen so it isn't a wall. "I'd like to do two things. One, keep your meds steady. Two, get a baseline on memory and attention. Not today. Short screen next week with the nurse."

Art's jaw squares. "I'm not a child."

"Neither am I," Dr Malik says. "It's a baseline. Helps us notice change if it comes when it comes."

Art looks at Joy. She does not answer for him.

"Fifteen minutes," the doctor says. "Numbers, words, a clock."

Art snorts. "Clocks I can do."

What does he mean?

"Good," the doctor says as if he is addressing a toddler. He prints the slip and hands it to Joy. "Next Wednesday, nine ten. Tell me if that time is bad."

"It's fine," Art says.

How do you know?

"Second thing," Malik goes on. "Men's morning at the hall. Tools, repairs. You tried it?"

"Twice."

"How was it?"

"The tools are blunt," Art says. "But the blokes are all right."

"Go again," Malik says. "Call it physiotherapy for the social muscles. Two hours a week."

Art's almost smiles. "I can manage that."

"Good." He types, then stops typing. "Any driving?"

"Short runs," Art says.

"Keep them short," Malik says. "Daylight. No new routes. If you get turned around, pull over. Phone home."

Art nods.

"Anything else worrying either of you?" Malik asks, still facing Art.

"No," Art says.

"Later," Joy says. "We'll bring the later when it's later."

"Do," Malik says. "That's the work."

She gives the slip to Art. He puts it in his pocket. In the car he touches it twice to make sure it's still there.

"Baseline?" he says.

"Yes."

"Pointless."

"Maybe, we'll see" she says. "Still useful. For later."

He looks out the window. "I'll do it."

"Good thinking."

At home she does not write it on the calendar. She takes her notebook to the small room and gives the appointment a single line: *Screen—Wed 9:10.*

At lunch he says: "Hall Tuesday."

"Ten."

"Dale?"

"If he wants."

He nods. After, he goes to the shed and stays. Later, he brings in a hinge screwed to a scrap of pine as if to prove he is still in the trade.

"Straight," he says.

"It is," she says.

She puts the slip in a clear sleeve with the other papers and closes his folder. That will do. She tells him his file is in the hallway sideboard.

In bed she is ball of fire. She is surprised by the force of her rage. It's like a hurricane. *How can he not feel it? How can he be so blunt? Blunt like the tools in the hall. He deserves them.*

18

A Small Bridge

Rain overnight. A clean edge to the air. He is at the table with the easy page of the crossword and a pencil he won't sharpen. It hardly writes anymore. She does not help.

A knock. Dale, holding a chair with a loose back rail. "You got glue?"

"In the shed," Art says. They go out.

Joy stays inside. She hears the small noises: clamp, tap, the drawer that sticks, the thud of the mallet used properly. She does the flat hand drumming. It keeps down the rage. She can hear what they are saying. They must've kept the shed door open or opened the window.

"Glue?" Dale asks.

"PVA," Art says. "Fine for this."

"Right."

She looks at the shed window. It is open indeed. They work. Dale holds, Art runs the bead, wipes squeeze-out with a rag that remembers other jobs. Clamps on. A check with the square. Quiet approval.

"Dowels?"

"Sound."

"Leave it an hour."

"Two," Art says.

Joy makes tea and puts two mugs on the bench. She does not carry them out. After five minutes Dale appears, takes them, nods a thanks, and goes back.

"Next Tuesday?" Dale says.

"Hall," Art answers.

"Before or after?"

"After."

"If breakwater's rough."

"The oval then."

"Right."

Joy stays at the table and writes three lines she won't hate tomorrow: *glue, clamp, leave.* It is enough. She can build on it later.

Two hours later the clamps come off. Dale rocks the chair lightly. It holds.

"Better than it was," Art says.

Dale looks at the hinge on the back gate. "That's gone."

"Needs a spacer," Art says.

"Got offcuts?"

"In the tin."

They fit a piece. Two screws. Done.

At the door Dale says, "You bring anything to the hall?"

"Hands," Art says.

"Bring that square," Dale says. "They don't own one."

"All right."

Dale nods at Joy. "See you."

"Thanks," she says.

When Dale's gone, Art stands a little taller. He rinses his mug and leaves it close enough to straight.

"Good morning?" she says.

He looks at her. Confused. "Work," he says.

After lunch he goes back out and sands the edge of the chair he didn't have to sand. A small finish, done for its own sake. Near four, he says, "I'll ring Dale next time."

"You can."

He picks up the phone, sets it down, picks it up again, dials. "Tuesday," he says into it. "After the hall." Pause. "Oval." Pause. "Right." He hangs up. "Sorted," he says.

"Sorted," she agrees.

She writes nothing on the calendar. The chair dries. The gate swings. That is the day. He turns the light off on her. She sits with her face in her hands, shaking her head.

Her expansion is explosive, leaving colours all around her. She stares into the kaleidoscope. *What am I supposed to do? Or not do? How can I go on? How long?* She dreams of leaving her body and flying above the roofs. On Ruth's roof is a single red shoe.

19

Baseline Test

Wednesday. Nine ten.

Reception, then the nurse's room. A table. Two chairs. A clipboard. The nurse smiles. "Just you," she says to Art. "Fifteen minutes."

Joy sits in the waiting area with a closed magazine in her lap. The clock ticks. She keeps her hands and face still. This is not easy. She can hear what's going on inside anyway.

"Tell me three words. Apple. Table. Penny."

He repeats them. "Apple. Table. Penny."

"Spell WORLD backwards."

"D... L... R... O... W." Slow but clean.

"Subtract seven from a hundred and keep going."

"Ninety-three... eighty-six... seventy-nine... seventy-two." He stops, frowns, finds sixty-five.

"Draw a clock. Set it to ten past eleven."

Silence while he draws the circle, the numbers tucked too close to the top. The hands point. Ten past eleven is legible.

"Name these." A pen lid. A watch. He names both.

"Copy this." Two intersecting pentagons. His lines meet, not perfectly.

"Tell me those three words again."

He gets two. "Apple... Penny." The third doesn't come. He looks at the table as if it might help. It doesn't.

"All right," the nurse says, opening the door. "Nearly done. Any trouble with steps? Getting lost? Stove?"

"No," he says.

"Sometimes," Joy says from the doorway, "Up the stairs is slow."

The nurse notes, nods. "Doctor will look it over. We'll ring."

Outside, cold air and the sound of a bin truck. He folds the results sheet he wasn't given and puts nothing in his pocket. Taps it twice.

For God's sake!

"How was it?" she asks.

"Childish," he says. A beat. "Fine."

"Coffee?"

"Home."

They drive back the short way. He takes his seat, opens the paper he wasn't given, reads it like a toddler would. Explains something about democracy. She doesn't listen. Says: "Good." She puts the kettle on and then turns it off. She wipes the bench once and stops. She doesn't reach for the calendar. This is not easy. *Will he make the coffee?* He doesn't.

At eleven, Dale texts: *Hall ?*

Art reads it and types: *Yes.* He shows her the screen.

"Good," she says.

After lunch he goes to the shed and planes an edge. She looks at him through the window. Shavings curl, pale. He holds the board up to the light and checks for straight. "True," he says. She reads his lips.

She writes one line in her notebook: *Apple, table . . .* She leaves the third word blank on purpose. She will remember why.

Late afternoon, the clinic rings. "Doctor says thank you for doing the screen. We'll review at your next visit. Keep routines. Call if anything changes."

"Thanks," she says. She hangs up. She does not translate any of it into a list.

Evening is plain. Frozen meals. Dishes. Kitchen floor. News. He puts a coaster under his glass. Before bed he says, "It was penny."

"It was," she says.

He nods once, satisfied, and turns off the light on her. She sits, face in her hands, shaking her head. *Why am I not crying?*

In bed she tries to cry. She does not succeed. It is as if her body stretches. Long, longer, longest. Sleep claims her. In a kind way. At least she has that.

20

The Detour

Saturday he wants screws. "Short run," he says.

She hands him the keys, his phone and the card with their number on it. He has a slip of paper in his pocket saying *screws*.

"Back in half an hour."

"Half an hour," she repeats.

He goes. The Ute coughs, catches.

She wipes the bench once and leaves the cloth where it falls.

Roadworks have closed the usual turn. A yellow arrow sends him right instead of left. He obeys, then obeys again, and ends in a street where all the trees look like each other. Conifers. He slows. He signals to no one and pulls into the servo. Inside: coffee machine, hotbox, a rack of air fresheners shaped like trees. The attendant greets him. "You right?"

"Detour," he says. He shows a card from his pocket. "Need this one."

"Ah," the attendant says. "Back to the highway, past the school, first left after the footy oval. You'll see the big blue sign."

Art nods. He walks out, stops, walks back. "Where's the school?"

"Follow the kids' crossing," the attendant says. "Zebra stripes. Can't miss."

Art nods, slower. He takes his phone from his pocket, looks at it, puts it back. He stands by the rack of wiper blades as if they might tell him something. Then he dials.

"Detour," he says when she answers. "At the servo."

"Stay there," she says. "I'll meet you."

"No," he says. "Tell me the turn after the oval again."

"Left," she says. "Blue sign."

"Right," he says. He hangs up before she can say more.

He returns to the ute, watches for the crossing, finds the oval, finds the blue sign. The left feels wrong. The hardware appears. He parks as if nothing happened. Inside, he asks for No. 8 x 30s and gets them, plus a packet he doesn't need but fits in his hand. He pays with notes that come out in the right order.

"Big day?" the cashier asks out of habit.

"Little one," he says.

Home within the hour. He places the screws on the table in their bag like proof. "Detour," he says.

"You found it."

"Servo helped." He puts the bag in the drawer with the other bags and aligns them once, then lets them sit crooked.

Will you ever form a proper sentence again?

After lunch he uses two screws and returns the driver to the tray without tapping . He stands in the doorway and looks at the ute.

She goes to the small room and adds a line: *Left after the oval. Blue sign. No sentences.* She stops there.

In the late afternoon the roadworks crew removes one barricade and leaves another. He takes a slow walk to the corner and back and doesn't report on it. She doesn't ask.

Evening is easier than usual. She does not know why. *Have I turned a corner? Can I be all right with this?*

Her expanding is less volatile. A quiet filling, like a huge balloon. Her breath seems to go on forever. *Ruth is right. I can do anything.*

21

Blackout

Just after six the lights go. A soft click, then the house without its hum. She waits. Nothing returns.

"Fuse?" he says.

She looks at Ruth's windows. Dark. "Outage," she says. She takes the torch from the drawer. He finds the second one in the laundry. The beams cross.

"Dinner?"

"Cold," she says. "Cheese. Bread."

They eat at the bench. The torches lie on their sides. Outside, rain holds steady. Somewhere a transformer pops like a far clap. He opens the meter box with the short key and stands, torch in teeth. "All down," he says. "Not us."

"Told you so."

They leave the box. Back inside, the dark settles.

"Candles?" he asks.

"No, only torches," she says.

He does not argue.

Ruth knocks once and pushes the door with her hip. "Yours out too?"

"Yes."

"Ruth lifts a camping lantern. "Spare, if you want."

"We're right," Joy says. "Keep it."

Ruth tips a hand. "Call if you need hot water. My stove's gas." She leaves the lantern anyway, on the mat, and goes.

They sit. No TV, no fan, no small noises stitching time. He taps the arm of the chair. "Quiet," he says.

"It is." *Stop tapping.*

He stands, puts on his coat, and steps to the back door. She follows to the threshold and no further. The yard is a cut-out: hedge, washing line, path, gate.

"Stars," he says.

"Clouds," she says.

He points. "Gap." A thumb-length clear patch opens and slides. The Southern Cross shows itself. He names it. He does not mention the other two he knew once. They stand a minute. *Like in the olden days.* Cold noses, wet cuffs. He returns in first. She shuts the door. He places the torches on the bench, beams up. They don't speak. She feels a surge of hope.

After a while he says, "Board games?" and smiles at the old word.

"Not tonight."

"Tomorrow?"

"Maybe, we'll see."

He nods.

A ute moves on the street and slows and moves again. Someone shouts "Back on soon" to no one in particular.

"Batteries?" he asks.

"Top drawer."

He finds them by feel, checks dates, puts two in the torch that flickered, leaves the old ones in the bowl with the keys for recycling. "Sorted," he says. He slices an apple in four neat quarters and leaves the knife flat on the board. They eat.

The power returns like a tide, not all at once. Fridge. Hall light. The clock blinks 12:00, ready to be taught again. He turns the nearest switch off so the room stays as it was. "Too bright," he says.

"For now," she says.

They put the torches back. She leaves the lantern Ruth brought on the mat. He returns it to the step, then thinks, and carries it across the street. Ruth opens her door as if she had been standing behind it. "On?" she asks.

"On," he says.

She takes the lantern and taps his sleeve. "Nice stars."

"Gap," he says, and gestures a thumb-length, and Ruth grins. "Northern light."

"Southern Cross," corrects Ruth.

"Ah yes."

He comes back. She sets the clock.

"Tea?" he asks.

"Tea," she says.

They stand by the bench while the jug finds its noise again.

"Next time candles?" he says, sounding hopeful.

"Maybe, we'll see" she says. "If we're careful."

He puts his cup in the rack. He turns two lights off and leaves one on. The house has resumed its hum. *Has he become aware?* She hears his rhythmic climb to the bedroom. Her legs refuse to follow him. She sits there, arms on the table. After a while she puts her face on her arms, expands and falls asleep. She is stone cold when she awakes with a jolt. She was young in her dream and running. Now she is old again. And Art . . . Accepting the unacceptable, she walks up the stairs.

He is sleeping with his mouth open. He looks dead.

22

The Notice

Wednesday, on the club board behind the glass, a new A4 with a black border. *Graham Fletcher — Service Friday 11.* A rink allocation sheet sits under it. She reads it once. An electric current shoots through her. Death.

He reads the first line and stops. "Fletch," he says.

Back home she says, "We can go. Or send flowers."

"Go," he says and she feels a rare surge of love for him.

She puts Friday's shirt on its hanger on the door. Sunday's shoes by the back door. He does not have to be asked to shine them. *Death motivates him more than anything.*

Ruth knocks in the afternoon. "Saw the notice," she says. "You going?"

"Yes."

"I'll give you a lift if you want company," Ruth offers. "I'll sit at the back and be useful or invisible."

"Thank you," Joy says. "We'll drive the ute."

Friday is clear. They arrive early and take a pew at the edge. The crematorium smells chemical. People settle into rows. A man from the committee hands out service sheets. Art holds the sheet but doesn't look at it. He watches the front. A photo of Graham at thirty, hat crooked, sits on a small easel.

The minister starts. *Is he even speaking English?* Joy tries to concentrate.

A daughter reads a note about her father's shed and the exact way he cut lengths.

Two mates from the club talk about a delivery that swung too wide in '98 and still gets a laugh. People laugh.

Joy watches Art's hands. They are quiet on his knees, which is rare. They are old hands. Strange hands. When the daughter says *patient*, he nods. When a hymn begins he doesn't open his mouth.

There is a photo roll. Fishing lines, Christmas hats, a steak on a grill. At the end, Graham older, still himself around the eyes.

Art inhales noisily.

After, on the lawn, people stand with cups. Vapour shows when they talk.

Len touches Art's elbow. "He was a good skip."

"Steady," Art says.

"Steady," Len agrees.

A woman Joy half knows says: "Hard times."

Joy says, "Yes."

Dale arrives from the car park, late. "Sorry," he says to no one. "Traffic." He stands with them and lets the breeze be the conversation.

When people begin to turn towards their cars, Art says, "Wake?" The word is strangely old-fashioned.

"Tea room," Joy says. "Biscuits." *I do not speak in sentences anymore either.*

He accepts a lukewarm cup and a triangle sandwich. He eats the sandwich. He leaves the cup half full.

A man she doesn't recognise says: "You were at Tech with him, weren't you?"

Art frowns. Joy doesn't fill the space.

"Bowls then," the man says. "You kept him honest on weight."

"He kept me straight on his line," Art says. The two men nod.

Ruth appears by the table with the biscuits. "You all right?"

"We are," Joy says.

Ruth takes a Monte Carlo. "He was a decent sort."

"He was," Joy says. The past tense bites.

They leave when the room begins to fill with chairs scraping, coats, a child asking about the box at the front.

In the car, he looks up at the gum leaves.

At home he goes to the shed. The mallet sounds once—soft—then stops. He comes back with a roll of sandpaper and sits at the table and tears it into strips measured by his thumb. He stacks them neatly. "Good turnout," he says.

"It was."

"Daughter spoke well."

"She did."

He places the sandpaper stack just so and then misaligns it by a few millimetres, on purpose or not. He leaves it.

Is he becoming sloppy at last?

In the afternoon he stands at the back step and looks at the strip she fitted weeks ago. "Fletch wouldn't have bothered," he says. *What is he saying?*

"He would have," she says.

"If you'd told him to."

Huh Has he lost the plot?

When Dale knocks at four, he doesn't ask for a walk. He hands over a small tin of screws. "From Graham's shed," he says. "Family's clearing."

Art takes them and does not open the lid. "Ta."

"Put them to work," Dale says.

"Will," Art says.

After Dale leaves, Art sets the tin on the kitchen bench, touches the lid once.

She heats a simple meal. He eats with the even chew that drives her wild, and at the end he says, "We should go Wednesday."

"To the hall?"

"To the green," he says. "Throw a few."

"Okay."

He rinses his plate. He taps the tin of screws on the bench. Before bed he moves it to the shelf above the sink where he will see it in the morning.

In the dark he says, "He had a good arm."

"He did."

"Kept his head."

"Yes."

Sleep comes differently, with a space made for someone else's absence, a bubble in her expansion. A surge of fear shoots through her.

23

A Few Ends

Wednesday holds. He says "Green?" at ten and again at one. At one-thirty she puts his shoes by the chair. He finds them with his feet. *Come on!* He pulls up his socks. He ties his shoes. Pulls up his socks. Chin at the ceiling.

"Are you in pain?" she asks, adamant to use a full sentence.

They walk in. The winter sun sits low, the green shows its seams. Len is there, Dale is there, two others from midweek roll. They say G'day.

"Three ends?" Dale asks.

"Three," Art says.

They set a mat on the spare rink. Art stands on the mat and looks down the line the way he always did. The first bowl runs long, then holds, then dies just outside the box. He makes a face.

"Green's quick," Len offers.

"Cold makes it honest," Art says.

What is he saying? What does that even mean? Has he always said that?

Second bowl pulls up short. He adjusts. Third sits near enough. He steps back, not quite pleased. They trade ends.

Dale rolls with his usual competent shoulder.

Len mutters about his knee and sends down something better.

The new bloke, Pete, throws one that hums and then lies down. No one claps. Midweek etiquette is to notice and not comment.

On the second end Art miscounts bowls and reaches for a fourth. Joy says nothing.

Dale taps his elbow and nods at the bag. "That's yours," he says.

Art grunts and rolls the white. Good length.

They carry on. A breath of wind slides across. A magpie comes down and changes its mind. The greenkeeper crosses with a bucket. On the third end Len steps into a small rut and catches himself. He laughs. "Old legs," he says.

"Mat's skew," Art says, and straightens it by millimetres.

They start the end again. At the measure Dale reaches for the string, stops, and hands it to Art. Art kneels slower than last month, lines the markers, breathes, reads it. "Yours," he says to Len, and the call is clean. Len nods.

They stop at three. No tally. Hands in pockets against the thin air.

"Next week?" Dale says.

"Next week," Art says.

Pete nods at the bag. "You coming Saturday?"

"Maybe, we'll see," Art says.

On the way out, the board behind glass still carries the black border. Art taps it with his finger.

Joy hurries past him trying to ignore the tapping.

Back home he takes the tin of Graham's screws from the shelf and opens it. Slot heads, Phillips, a few brass. He tips ten into his palm, sorts them by habit, returns nine, leaves one on the bench.

"What's that for?" she asks.

"Later," he says.

He goes to the shed and looks at the chair he already fixed and keeps carrying back and forth. He doesn't touch it. He picks up the square he promised to bring to the hall and checks it on the edge of the bench though he knows it's true. He sets it beside the bag in the hallway.

Dale knocks once and puts his head in. "Good roll," he says.

"Average," Art says.

"Average is honest," Dale replies. He looks at the tin. "Fletch's?"

"Family sent them," Art says.

"Use them," Dale says.

Art smiles with half his mouth. *Has he had a stroke? One of these mini things? Since when is his smile lopsided?*

Dale goes.

Joy makes tea and sets a mug at the far corner of the bench. He fetches it later and drinks half, cold. *As if he's hard at work.* He places the empty mug near the sink and leaves it.

After, she takes a walk to the corner alone. The cold bites her nose and clears it. When she comes back he has the square in the bag and the bag by the door. *Life is like a snail's journey now. Or like poop travelling through the body. Inch by inch.* He has put the screw from the bench into the small box that lives in the side pocket.

"Hall tomorrow?" she asks.

"Ten," he says. "Not if it's raining."

"It will still be there."

He shrugs.

Evening, Dale texts a photo from his back step: a cloud bank over the creek, a clean line. *Next Wed 2* is all he texts. Art reads it, looks at the sky through their window, types *2,* and puts the phone down.

They eat. She keeps calm. He moves the knife to the rack the right way up without being told. Later, he wipes a wet ring from the table with the flat of his palm, finds a tea towel, and does it properly. She says nothing.

Before bed she opens her notebook and adds four lines:

Three ends.
Mat straightened.
Measure called clean.
Screw saved for later.

She closes the book. He sets the bag by the door and taps it once, the quiet sound of a plan. She climbs the stairs behind him. He does not have a bottom anymore. It's hollow in his pyjama pants.

"You're too skinny," she says.

He is in defensive mode immediately. "Doc decides that."

"You have no bum left."

He mutters something she does not understand.

In bed she needs to dissociate from him and his body. It is not hard. It's like rounding a corner in her mind. She becomes large and radiant. She feels her apple-like cheeks glow, her eyes sparkle, her lips smile. That's how sleep finds her.

24

Checkout

Tuesday afternoon she says, "Shop?" and hands him the list. Small, block letters. Four items. "You must get out."

"Bread. Milk. Tomatoes. Soap," he reads.

They go to the supermarket with the short trolleys that steer like toys. The doors sigh them in. Heat from the vents hits and stops. He takes the first aisle by habit. *Cleaning.* He finds soap without looking at brands. Puts two in. "Better to have," he says. She doesn't edit. *Sure, we'll only have twelve or so soon, like the toothbrushes.*

Fruit's next. He touches three tomatoes, picks the fourth, checks the weight in his hand. He bags a couple of them. He looks up at the misting nozzles and steps back. "Did they have these last time?"

She doesn't answer.

Bread. He chooses the sliced with the square corners because it fits the tin. He tucks it under his arm the way he used to carry off-cuts. Milk is at the far end. He lifts a two-litre, swaps it for one with a better date. He sets it upright in the trolley. At the screws aisle, not on the list, he pauses. A man in a hi-vis jacket is frowning at packets. "Need eight by thirty," the man mutters.

"Top row," Art says, not loud. "Second from the edge."

The man reaches, finds them, holds the packet up like he's won something. "Cheers."

Art almost-smiles. *Again lopsided.* They move on. At the end of the aisle, Graham's daughter is there by the specials bin. No hat. She sees them. A twitch at the corner of her mouth that could be a smile. Joy says, "We were there Friday."

"Thank you," the daughter says. "He liked you."

"Steady skip," Art says.

"He was," the daughter says. She touches the oranges in her basket as if to check they're real. Her fingers are restless and pale. They part. Checkout. He chooses a person, not a machine. The boy scans. Beep, beep, beep. Bread flattens.

"Don't flatten it," she says. The boy stops flattening it. "Bags?"

"Two," Art says, and counts them with his eyes.

Tap time. He takes out the card, turns it the wrong way, turns it right. The machine chirps. For a second he doesn't move.

"Done," the boy says, kindly.

Art nods and puts the card away. Outside, the trolley hits the lip and jars. He catches the milk with one hand. "Got it," he says.

He moved like he used to. She feels a surge of love for him.

He loads the ute with extreme neatness and slowness. He returns the trolley to the rack that never sits straight, nudges it in until it behaves.

Home, he puts the milk left of the juice, bread in the tin, tomatoes on the bench, soap under the sink. No asking where. No wrong doors. He leaves the list on the table. Four ticks. A small square drawn around them.

"Good run," she says.

"Straightforward," he says.

She halves a tomato for lunch, salt on the cut faces.

He eats his half. "Saw Graham's girl," he says.

"She's all right."

"She is," he says.

After, he takes the spare soap to the shed and stores it on a shelf with old paint and rags.

She writes one line: *Person, not machine. Too much soap.* Then stops.

In the evening he turns off the light on her. She sits in the dark for a while. It wasn't a bad day. She even felt love.

She walks up the stairs. Dread fills her. If only I could sleep alone.

On the mattress, as far from his body as possible, she closes her eyes and expands. *Here I go.*

25

Licence

Mail at ten. A windowed envelope with the blue band. *VicRoads — Medical review.*

She sets it on the table. He comes in, reads his name, opens it with the care. She observes him without really recognising him. "Driver licence medical," he reads. "GP report within four weeks. Eye test. If not, licence may be suspended." He finds the date. He finds it again.

"We'll book Malik," she says.

"I drive fine," he says.

"You do short runs in daylight," she says. "This keeps that."

He folds the letter once, then twice.

She rings the clinic. "Soonest with Dr Malik?"

Why have I started doing things for him again? When did I start?

"Next Thursday, eleven twenty."

"We'll take it."

He puts the letter on the sideboard.

After lunch he moves the Ute forward and back in the driveway. He stops, leaves it straight, comes in.

"Glasses?" she asks.

"Good enough," he says.

"Take both," she says.

He shrugs.

Stop shrugging, please, please. If you shrug again, I don't know what I will do.

Ruth knocks later, sees the blue band on the letter. "Ah," she says. "Mine came at seventy-six. Made Ken swear at the kettle."

"He'll see Malik," Joy says.

Ruth nods. "Take biscuits. He'll hate it less."

He goes to the shed. On his way checks the little triangle on the tyre He wipes his hands.

Wednesday he drives to the green and back.

Thursday he doesn't drive.

Friday Dale knocks and says, "Need anything from Bunnings?"

Art says: "No," quickly, as if the offer was a test.

Like poop through the body. Inch by inch.

Saturday he takes the short run to the grocer. Bread, milk, soap are done; he buys oranges. There's a one-word list in his pocket. He returns on time and places them where fruit goes, where he can find them. She's puts the bowl somewhere else, as a test.

Sunday is quiet. He looks at the letter twice, taps it, then leaves it alone.

Monday she prints a small card: *Thursday 11:20 — licence medical — bring glasses.* She puts it under the magnet with the fish. He sees it, taps it once with two fingers.

On Thursday they go early. Reception. The foyer smells of gel and winter coats. Malik's room at eleven thirty. The doctor reads the letter before he looks up. He smiles without sympathy. "We'll do the form."

Vision first. Eye chart on the wall. "With glasses, please."

Art puts them on. Reads the top lines, slows near the smaller ones.

Malik says: "Now without."

The lines blur.

"With," Malik says. "You'll wear them," and ticks the box.

Strength. Grip. Ankles. A quick check of range. "Any dizzy?"

"No," Art says.

"Sometimes," Joy says.

"Not while driving," Art says, and Malik ticks.

Memory. "If you get turned around?"

"Servo, ask, phone," Art says. A beat. "Left after the oval. The blue light," he adds.

Malik ticks.

Medications — unchanged. Blood pressure — steady. "Short runs," Malik writes in the small boxes. "Daylight. No new routes. Review twelve months." He turns the form for signatures. "You understand the conditions," he says, facing Art.

"I do."

"Any questions?"

"No."

"I'll lodge this today," Malik says. "You'll get a letter. Keep the old card in the car until the new card comes."

Outside, the wind is clean and not entirely unfriendly. He exhale-laughs once. "Childish," he says.

"Done," she says.

They stop for two small pies at the bakery on the way back and share a flimsy table with a man and a map.

At home he puts the old glasses next to the lemon mug. He puts a copy of the letter in the glove box. He checks the tyres with a foot. In the afternoon he drives to the servo and back for no reason, parks straight, comes in, says nothing. She doesn't ask.

"Who uses maps still?"

She is surprised he remembers.

Ruth texts *All good?*

Joy writes back *Ticked.*

Of course, Ruth replies.

Dale calls. "Still on for two?"

"Yes," Art says.

They walk the oval because the wind at the breakwater is too crazy. On the far side Dale says, "Malik?"

"Ticked," Art says.

"Good," Dale says.

"Daylight," Art says.

"Daylight is good enough."

That night he takes the keys from the bowl, stands, and puts them back. After dinner he wipes the bench and leaves a small wet crescent. She leaves it to fade by itself.

In her notebook she writes one line: *Licence — daylight, short runs — twelve months*. She closes it.

Before sleep he says, to the ceiling, "Blue sign."

"Yes," she says.

"Left after the oval."

"Yes."

The house is dark and ordinary and holds them. No disasters have occurred. The keys are in the bowl. Tomorrow can be a drive to nowhere. He will choose. She will not choose for him. She holds her own heart in her hands and looks at it. It glistens. She offers it to an invisible audience. There is applause. She bows. There are flowers. She bows again.

26

The Wrong Gate

Late morning she hands him an envelope. Rates. "Post?"

"I'll walk." He takes the keys from the bowl and puts them back. Shoes. Coat, hat. He checks the letter twice.

Out and back is four streets and a crossing with the faded zebra. He drops the envelope twice. On the return the rain is a mist. Houses: hedge, fence, gum, brick. He turns in at a gate that looks right and is not. Same hedge height. Same letterbox, almost. A dog lifts its head and holds a note low in its throat.

"Art?" Ruth's voice from next door, flat, practical.

He stops. Looks at the path, the windows, the pot with the dead geranium.

"Yours," Ruth says, one finger to the left.

He backs out, shuts the gate, walks past Ruth to the next. Their latch clicks the way it always has. He touches it, nods once to himself, and goes in.

She is at the sink. He stands in the doorway.

"Next to Ruth's," he says. "I almost went in."

"Close enough," she says.

"Same hedge."

"Ours has rosemary."

He looks, sees the low green and the blue-grey behind it. "Right."

He hangs the hat.

After lunch she brings out the little stencil kit from the drawer and the tin of white. "Kerb?" she says.

"Number," he says.

They go to the verge. He tapes the edges, lays the stencil straight. He paints the digits with a careful hand that doesn't hurry. The white takes. He peels the card. The number sits there, clean.

"Mailbox too," he says. He ties a narrow strip of faded blue cloth around the post, a knot a carpenter would trust.

Ruth appears with her bin and stops. She says: "Yours looks like yours now."

Inside, he moves the small fish magnet an inch lower on the fridge door. She leaves it there.

In the afternoon he walks to the corner and back by himself because she pressured him to. At the gate he hesitates half a second, then lifts the latch on their side.

Later she writes three lines:

Wrong gate.

Rosemary, not just hedge.

Number white on kerb.

She shuts the notebook.

In the evening, he rinses a glass and sets it down. "Ruth caught me," he says, "at the other side of hers."

"She did."

"Good to have neighbours," he says.

"Yes."

He goes outside and taps the knot on the mailbox once on his way in from the dark. The latch clicks.

In bed the applause starts as soon as her head hits the pillow. It is deafening. She knows she deserves it. Flowers are thrown into her direction. Thick bunches of them.

27

The Cut

Saturday. Hair over the ears again. She says nothing. He looks in the mirror and says, "Barber?"

"Eleven."

They walk. The shop has three chairs, one working. A radio on low. Dead hair on the floor. A sign: *No appointments.*

"Next," the barber says. "Arthur?"

"Art," he says, and sits.

Cape. Paper at the neck. Mirror. "How're we doing?" the barber asks.

"Same."

"Number three sides, tidy top?"

Art nods.

The clippers start buzzing. He looks past himself, not at.

She looks at his mirrored image. *His face is lopsided. When did that start? Is he having these mini strokes?*

The barber talks weather and footy.

Art answers in single words. When asked about work he says "Shed."

"Chin down," the barber says.

He obeys.

"Eyebrows?"

"Leave them." A beat. "No, trim."

Snip. Guard off. A comb like a ruler taps the temple once. The barber lines the back with the small trimmer, wipes with a brush that smells like menthol.

"Still got it thick," the barber says.

"Stubborn," Art says.

It's true, his hair is still good. She feels a surge of love.

Cape off. A dusting at the collar. He stands carefully, slower than last time. At the till he takes out his card, gets the angle right the first time.

"All good, Art," the barber says. "See you in six."

"Four," Art says.

The barber smiles.

Outside, she waits with a small bag from the bakery. He tips his head. *The cut looks like him.*

"Pie?" she says.

"Half."

They sit on the bench by the chemist and share. It's almost like it once was. A boy rides past on a scooter. A dog pulls a lead. The wind lifts the napkin and he pins it with one finger without looking. He checks his head in the shop windows as they pass. The line at the back is clean. "Straight," he says.

"Yes, neat," she agrees.

Back home he takes the broom and clears the laundry floor. *Why? Is he clearing the hair?* He hangs the shirt he wore to the shop and chooses another.

"Hang that one outside so that the hairs can leave it."

He does what she says. *Thank God.*

After lunch he goes to the shed and oils the hinge on the back gate. "Squeaks," he says.

She writes one line: *Art, not Arthur.* Then closes the notebook.

Near evening Brendan texts: *Looks sharp, Dad.* A photo must have gone round without her seeing it.

Art types: *Cut. All good.*

Brendan replies with a thumbs up.

At the sink he runs a hand over the edge and finds no snag. He leaves the hand there a second longer, then reaches for a glass.

"Next time four," he says.

"Four," she says. She has no idea what he's on about.

He nods. He sets the glass down.

She's been to the counsellor again. She suspects he's as lonely as she is. Different, but lonely anyway. She goes over the stages of grief in her mind. Denial, anger, bargaining, depression, and acceptance. *I'm stuck in anger.* The counsellor said: it rolls like it rolls. She wonders if she should give it up. She is not progressing. *Anger. Rage. Fury. What's the point.*

In bed, applause washes over her. The smell of fresh flowers. Her cheeks glow, her lips feel alive. Her chest rises and falls. She squeezes the muscles on her upper arms. Then opens her arms wide. Gratitude washes over her. *I am alive.*

28

The Card

Mail at ten again. A small white envelope, plastic lump inside. *VicRoads.* He opens it at the table. New licence. The photo flatters. She feels a surge of love when she looks at it. Under conditions: *Daylight only. Local area.* He reads the line twice.

"Keep the old one?" he asks.

"Bin," she says.

Does he even notice we do not use sentences anymore?

He drops the expired card into the shred tin and turns the handle. The strip curls. "Done".

He takes the new one to the ute, sits in the driver's seat, slides it into the wallet slot. He checks the glove box for the copy letter. Back inside he sets the letter on the sideboard in the hallway together with the screws tin.

Mara rings after lunch. "We're short a square," she says. "Can you bring yours Thursday?"

"Yes," he says.

"Ten," she says.

"Ten," he repeats.

He hangs up and does not look to Joy for translation.

Wednesday he drives the short run to the green and back, daylight, the usual way. No report.

She doesn't ask.

Thursday, square in the bag. They walk. Rain holds off. At the hall he places the square on the bench and taps it once.

Ed says: "Good one."

Dale holds a plank up and finds centre.

The boy with the stool from last week brings a drawer with a swollen side. "Can you plane it?" he asks.

Art shows him how to check the grain. The boy watches. Art explains at length. Three passes. The drawer slides.

Mara drifts past. "You all right to show him again next week?" she asks Art.

"Yes," he says.

Joy goes to the bakery. She sits without writing and counts buses for five minutes like Ruth told her to. She returns at twelve. They pack up on the clap. Outside, near the crossing, the new neighbour is at the fence with a dog that doesn't bark. "Art," he says. "Work on the gate."

Art's mouth tries 'Alan' and finds it. "Alan," he says.

Alan grins. "Thought I'd have to chase that hinge all winter."

"Spacer," Art says. "Two screws."

"Shows," Alan says, pleased.

They part. *Another one worder.*

Home, he sets the square on the sideboard again instead of back in the bag. "Tomorrow," he says, though there's nothing booked. After lunch he goes to the shed and planes the edge of a random piece of wood. Three curls, then he stops. He returns the plane to the shelf, sole down.

Ruth knocks once and looks at the licence on the sideboard. "Daylight," she reads. "Local. Reasonable."

"Better than none," Joy says.

Ruth says: "He'll live longer."

Is that a good thing or a bad thing?

Evening. He puts the keys from his pocket in the bowl.

Before bed, in the dark, she writes a single line: *Card in wallet. Square on bench. Alan by name.* Then closes the notebook.

She turns away from the applause. It is in her back now. Like a strong wind. She walks away from it. Opens her arms once again. Turns. People stand. Applause changes in rhythmic clapping. More more more. *More of what?* She has forgotten what she is here for on this stage. Fear slams through her. She sits up and finds the evening, the house. Art sleeps with his mouth open. His face looks dead above the striped collar. A trail of spit had dried on his cheek. She watches in silent horror. Then sleep takes her, compassionate.

29

Library Afternoon

Tuesday. Returns in a bag. She says "Library?"

He nods.

Inside, heating that smells like dust. The desk bell is a rubber pad. A girl with a nose ring scans the books and sets them in a straight pile that will not hold.

"Large print came in," the girl says. "Joy?"

"Yes." She slides two across. Joy takes one. Leaves one.

Art wanders to the magazines. He stands too close, then steps back. He picks up the one with sheds on the cover, flips, stops at a page with a bench plan. He taps a picture once.

On the wall, a small local history: school photos, flood of '74, a plaque from the old hall.

He reads two captions. One lands. "Merv Garton," he says. "Left-hander." The name arrives whole. He doesn't wait for praise. She doesn't give it.

At the desk, her card doesn't read. The girl turns it, tries again. "Chip's sulking," she says. "I'll put it through manual." Pen on paper. Signature. Done.

Art brings the magazine to the desk and leaves it there. "Bench is wrong," he tells the air. "Vice's on the left."

"Noted," the girl says, smiling.

They sit by the window. Rain finds the glass. A small boy at the next table whispers spelling to himself and gets stuck. Art says, to Joy, not to the boy, "Two Ls." The boy hears it anyway and writes it. *He notices things; only not the right ones.*

Joy opens the large print. She reads one page. Closes it. Opens the notebook and writes three short lines: *shed plan, name on the plaque, chip that sulked.*

He goes to the catalogue computer and touches the screen with one finger. He types planes and gets planets. He backspaces. Tries again. Finds a book from 1983 with a cover that has not aged. He finds it on the shelf, checks two drawings, puts it back.

At the exit he sets the bag down and looks around. *Okay, now what?*

Cold air.

"Coffee?" she asks.

He says: "Short one."

They share one at the bakery corner. *Like in the olden days. Does he remember?* She does not ask.

He watches the bus swing wide and clear the curb by a clean inch. "Good driver," he says.

Home, he puts the bag on the table, takes the magazine out, places it cover up. He goes to the shed and comes back with the small vice and sets it on the bench, left side. He leaves it there like a reminder.

A reminder of what?

She writes one line: *Merv Garton — left-hander. A reminder.* Stops.

In the late afternoon he moves the fish magnet back up a notch without comment. He rinses a glass and sets it down. She leaves it. *Like poop through a body. Inch by inch. Every day the same. Every night true.*

Evening, the phone pings. Brendan: *All good?*

Art types: *Library. Pie.* Sends.

Brendan: *Nice.*

Nothing else. *Is that all?*

Before bed she puts the library receipt in the drawer that doesn't stick. He taps the vice once on his way past, a small metal sound that means nothing.

In bed, she walks away from the applause that hits her in the back like a strong wind. It pushes her forward. Her feet leave the ground. She floats above the stage, the red shoes limp on her feet. Her eyes are moist. *Am I crying at last?*

30

The Map

Morning's plain. He says, "Servo?" and doesn't take the keys. "Later," she says. "Paper first."

After lunch she brings an old envelope and a biro to the table. "Map," she says.

He looks at the blank side. Waits.

"Start here." She draws their street as a line with a square for the house. A small cross for Ruth. "Hall." A block with a door. "Library." A rectangle with a window. "Oval." A loop. "Servo." A star. "Hardware." A box with a blue bar.

He takes the pen. Adds the breakwater with three short wavy strokes. Puts a dot where the bakery sits. Draws the creek as a thin bend. He prints names in the tidy caps he taught.

"Left after the oval," he says, and writes left along the turn. He draws the crossing stripes by the school. He marks the gate with a small triangle and adds theirs.

She doesn't correct anything. She keeps her hands still. This is not easy.

He studies the lines. "Back way?"

"Show it."

He sketches the second route to the hardware—the one that bypasses the detour and the school. Two turns only. He writes *short* beside it. He adds the hall clock tower with a square tooth. The library case with a tiny plaque. The bench outside the chemist with a straight line for the back.

Ruth knocks once and leans in. Sees the envelope. She says: "Make two."

He draws the same again, simpler. Fewer marks. Just the left turn, the oval, the blue bar. He writes *SPARE* on the corner. He folds it and slides it into his wallet behind the card.

"Phone photo," Ruth says. He places it on the table. She takes the picture for him. "No shadow, no glare, see?" Done.

He looks at the first map a long time. "Clock this way," he says, and adds an arrow by the hall. He scratches it out, redraws it. "No. That way." He taps the arrow when it's right.

He stands. "Test?"

"Go."

He takes the keys. Wallet, map, envelope. He repeats the turns under his breath. The ute coughs, catches. He goes.

She does not stand at the window. She sets the kettle on, wipes one square of bench and stops. She sits. Ten minutes. Twelve. A car door. The keys in the bowl. He comes in with screws he didn't need and oranges. *Oranges again.*

"Back way works," he says. "Blue sign faded." He shrugs. "Still blue."

He sets the spare map on the sideboard in the hallway, next to the tin of screws. He tapes the other one, small, inside the hall cupboard where the jackets hang. Not on the fridge. *Why?*

Dale texts: *Wed 2 still?*

Art types: *Still.* He does not show her the phone.

She writes two lines:

Map on an envelope.

Left after the oval, twice.

Late afternoon he moves the fish magnet back down. He straightens the envelope's edge and then leaves it crooked again. She moves the bowl of oranges to the windowsill.

Evening, Brendan pings: *Proud of you, Dad.*

Art replies: *Made map.*

Brendan sends a heart.

Before bed, he taps the door once where the map sits. "Tomorrow," he says.

"It will be there," she says. He goes up the stairs. She does not watch. *Where can I go? What can I do? The counsellor is as lonely as I am. What is the point?*

When her head hits the pillow, she's floating. A wind made of clapping hands and admiring voices is carrying her. She looks out over the town, floats higher and higher, toward a golden light.

31

The Leak

Midnight. A soft tap that isn't branches. Then another. She wakes to damp on the carpet by the wardrobe. The world is ugly after the golden light. *What was that about?*

"Roof," he says from the doorway, already up.

"Bucket first," she says.

Laundry bucket. Towel. She moves the shoes. He touches the ceiling with two fingers as if feeling for a pulse.

"Centre," he says.

She sets the bucket under it. The next drop finds the middle cleanly. He stands a minute, mapping joists he can't see.

"Ladder," he says.

"Not now."

"Now."

She weighs it. "Torch. Boots. No heroics."

He nods. Boots. She puts them by his feet. Old coat. He sticks his arms in the sleeves. Torch between his teeth, idiotic. She holds the ladder while he climbs to the eave. Rain's fine, not driving. The gutter lip overflows where leaves have collected.

"A block," he says.

"Gloves." She holds them up. Torch between teeth again.

He clears leaves, branches, a blue peg, one cork. He throws them onto the path. Water runs again the way it should. "Still," he says, listening. He shifts along the gutter. Another mound. Off. On. Flow changes and takes the pressure with it. A different sound.

"Good now," she says. He comes down carefully, much slower than last year, but boots steady on each rung. He points with the torch.

"Tomorrow," she says.

They go inside. A towel. A bucket catches the last drops, then it stops. She leaves it there anyway. He stands at the window, coat dripping. "Tape," he says. "Flashing."

"Daylight," she says.

He nods.

They do not go back to sleep. Tea in the kitchen. Coats over chairs. He lays the blue peg on the table between them. "Yours," he says.

"Ruth's," she says. "Her line's higher."

"Tell her."

Morning changes the rain into mist. He brings the ladder out again. She holds the feet. He goes to the valley with his hands, finds the old patch lifting. "Here," he says.

"Down," she says. "I'll get the kit."

Tape. Sealant. A handful of screws. The driver with a charged battery—she checked two weeks ago. He goes up again. She passes things by habit. They've done this many times. He presses the tape, screws a clip where it will not show. Sealant smooth with a gloved thumb. Old tricks remembered by his hands rather than by his brain.

"Test," she says, and tips a jug of water from the ladder's second step. The run is straight, decisive. No seep. The gutter takes it.

Inside, the towel is wet. The bucket redundant. She moves both. He lifts the carpet corner, checks the underlay with two fingers. "All right," he says.

Ruth appears with her bin and looks up at the roof. "Sorted?"

"Valley tape," he says.

"Pegs?" she asks.

"Yours," Joy says, and hands it over.

Ruth clips it to her sleeve. "Council would charge for that." She looks at the ladder. "Good angle," she says.

After lunch he goes back up once more. He comes down and hoses the leaves off the line. He coils the hose. "The bucket can retire," he says.

She writes three lines:

Block, peg, cork.

Valley tape.

Bucket retired.

He moves the ladder to the shed and leaves it open to dry. He oils the hinges on the way past, two drops each, a habit that costs nothing. At four he stands under the repaired patch and looks up. "Holds," he says.

"It holds," she agrees.

He eats with the even chew. *It's better when he has done things.* She leaves the dishes to drain and moves onto other chores. Before bed he taps the wall once with two knuckles, an old carpenter's test.

In the dark she thinks. *Maintenance.* Tomorrow she will check the ceiling again. But first she must fly. She looks down and sees him standing there, a tiny figure, on a ladder. She is at his feet, looking up. *Where is the light?*

32

The Folder

Morning's clear. She takes his folder from the drawer and lays it on the table. Clear sleeves. Dividers. Paper first, order later. Licence letter on top. Copy of the card underneath. GP list: *Malik; clinic; after-hours.* Hall phone. *Dale. Ruth. Alan.* She prints them in tidy caps, one line each.

"Sign here," she says, sliding a simple consent for information across. He reads the first line, the last line, signs.

"Hospital?" he asks.

"Just numbers," she says.

He says: "Numbers are fine."

What does he mean?

She adds the map—the envelope one—enlarged on the library copier to double-size. Tape at the corners so it won't slip inside the sleeve. She writes *Left after the oval* once in the margin. She will make several copies. Just in case. At the library, the copier sulks. She feeds coins, sets A4, presses start. The machine delivers the page in a curl that relaxes as it cools. Done.

Back home, she adds the *Not mine to do* card to a sleeve of its own. Not to show anyone. To remind herself. She doesn't label it. She keeps the folder on the sideboard where the screws tin sits. Visible, but not ostentatious. *Am I going crazy? Not him but I? Am I the one who is deteriorating?*

Ruth knocks. "One copy here. One there." She points at the bench. "I'll take phone numbers only."

Joy writes them on a card: *Malik, Dale, Hall, Clinic.*

Later, Ruth slides it under a magnet shaped like a tomato on her fridge.

After lunch Joy rings Brendan. "I'm making a folder," she says. "If you ever need it."

"Good stuff," he says. "Email it?"

"No," she says. "Paper and pen. In the house."

"Right. I'll remember."

"You won't," she says, without heat. "That's why it lives here."

He laughs once, caught and not offended. "Fair."

She prints one page: *If I'm not here.* Two lines only. *Call Ruth. Call Malik.* She puts it at the front.

He comes in from the shed with sawdust on his cuffs. Sees the sideboard. "My folder?" he says.

"Your folder."

He opens it to the map. "Left after the oval," he reads, recognising his own writing.

"Hall?" she asks.

"Tomorrow," he says.

At the hall, next morning, the boy returns with a plank. "It needs a straight cut," he says.

"Mark both sides," Art says. He embarks on a lengthy explanation while he shows the boy the knife line, shallow, twice. "Plane to it, not through." The boy nods and makes the cut.

Dale lifts the square. "Still true," he says.

"Still," Art says.

Joy sits at the bakery and writes two lines: *Folder on sideboard. Map enlarged.* She watches three buses pass.

The afternoon's cold. Home, she adds one last sheet: medication names printed, not nicknames, doses in numbers. She doesn't put his pills on the bench. She puts the paper in a sleeve. *Let's see if he fetches the pills himself.*

In the evening she moves the folder an inch to the left. He notices. Taps it once with two fingers. "There," he says.

"There," she says.

Before bed she writes one line in the notebook: *Not a plan. A place.* She closes it. Her mouth slowly opens wide. She is screaming but no sound comes out. Instead there are creatures and objects. They are all leaving her. They are expelled from her body. She has once seen a painting in a book by Marc Chagall. It is like that but different. When she wakes her cheeks hurt.

33

The Key Safe

Parcel at ten. Small box, heavy. *Key safe — wall mount.* She sets it on the table.

He reads the back: four screws, four digits. "Front step?" he says.

"Side wall," she says. "Under the eave."

They choose a spot where rain won't matter and hands will find it. He marks the brick with a pencil dot, four times. Drill, plugs, screws. He tightens until the plate sits flush but not strained.

"Code?" he asks.

"Not birthdays. Not street numbers," she says.

"Fletch," he says, then shakes his head. "No."

Why say 'no' when you have just shaken your head? Why do I not know you? Have I ever known you? Do I know myself? She writes four numbers that only make sense to them. He dials them, twice, until his fingers know. The door clicks open with a small sound.

Key choices are next. Not the ute. Not the shed. Front door only. She ties a short length of blue cloth to the ring, the same faded knot as the mailbox. He slides the key into the cavity and shuts the door. Tests. Open. Shut. Again.

Ruth knocks once. "Code?" she asks.

"I'll text you," Joy says.

"Don't," Ruth says. "Say it."

Joy says it.

Ruth nods, repeats it back without writing. "I'll forget until I need it, then I won't."

They agree on a rule: Ruth uses it only if asked, or if smoke, or if no answer and morning has turned to lunch.

Ruth says "Right" and leaves.

Dale knocks later. "Sensible," he says, looking at the plate. He does not ask the code.

Brendan texts in the afternoon: *Heard you put in a key safe. What's the code?*

She writes back: *We'll give it in person.*

I'm flat out, he replies.

Then later, she sends.

He calls at five. "Just tell me," he says, cheerful and tired at once.

"In person," she repeats. "We'll show you the spot."

A pause. "Right." He adjusts to the rule. "Soon."

After dinner Art goes out with a torch and opens the safe, shuts it, opens it again. "Works," he says.

"Side wall was right," she says.

He taps the eave where the drip line ends. "Dry," he says.

She adds a card to the folder: *Key safe — side wall. Code known to: Ruth, Brendan (when told).* She puts the card in a sleeve.

Next morning she tests without telling him. She steps out, shuts the door, uses the code, opens. Inside in ten seconds.

He glances up from the table and sees the door move. "Good?" he asks.

"Good."

At lunch Ruth knocks and lets herself in, announces "Testing," and stands inside the hall. "Still works," she says, and leaves again.

In the afternoon he adds a small screw through the bottom edge of the plate into brick. He wipes the dust with the side of his hand.

She writes one line: *Key safe—code in mouths, not on paper.* Stops.

In the evening he moves the keys to the bowl. Before bed he steps out and back once, using the safe in the dark, counting under his breath. The numbers fit. The latch clicks. The house admits him.

What an excitement! A key safe. Where's the time we danced away the night? She remembers his eyes on hers. Their foreheads touching. The glow between them. *This is how it ends. It is almost over.* A dry sob escapes her.

34

The Handover

Brendan comes at four on a Thursday, daylight thin. No text first. Ute, door, boots on path. "Two minutes," he says.

"Side wall," Joy says.

Art takes him out. Torch not needed yet. He taps the safe with two fingers. "Code?"

"Say it," Joy tells Brendan.

Brendan repeats the numbers.

Art dials them, slow, exact. The door clicks. He shows the blue tie on the ring. "Front only."

"Got it," Brendan says. He reaches for his phone. "I'll take a photo—"

"No," Joy says. "In your head."

He pockets the phone. "In my head only." He says the numbers again.

Inside, the folder sits on the sideboard. Joy opens it to the first sleeve. "Numbers. Map. Meds. If I'm not here—Ruth, Malik."

Brendan nods, quick. "Smart."

He flips, stops at the reduced map. "Left after the oval," he reads. "Back way if roadworks. Right."

"Don't take it," Joy says.

"I won't." He looks at Art. "Proud of you, Dad."

Art shrugs. "Local," he says. It covers more than driving.

Brendan turns to the screws tin. "Graham's?"

"Yes," Art says.

"Use them," Brendan says.

They stand in the kitchen. No kettle. No biscuits. Brendan looks at the clock. "I can do Saturday," he starts.

"Don't pencil it," she says. "Just come."

He exhales. "Right. I'll come." He moves to the door.

"Code again?"

He says it. Art says it with him. Joy says nothing. She looks at father and son.

At the gate Brendan hesitates. "Folder stays?"

"Here," she says.

"If I need it?"

"Ruth has numbers," she says. "You have the code."

He grins. "I'm trusted."

"You're instructed," she says.

Why am I so cold, so unkind?

He goes. The ute coughs, catches, leaves.

Art stands by the sideboard and taps the folder once. "There," he says.

"There," she agrees.

He puts the blue-tied key back in the safe and shuts the door without looking up. Inside ten seconds. Back in ten more.

She writes two lines:

Code said, not stored.

Brendan instructed, not deputised.

She closes the notebook.

She stays in the bathroom until he's moved upstairs. She cannot bear to look at his backside. The sharp shoulder blades, the no-bum. She hasn't seen him entirely naked in months. Maybe she should.

He's hiding it from me. She walks to the bed when she feels he's sound asleep. She flies high in the sky, like a kite. She's connected to her tiny body with a thin thread, like a kite. The thread is attached to her navel. *Am I dying?*

35

The Cold

She wakes wrong. Light-headed, heat behind her eyes. "Today is a no," she says to the room.

He hears the cough. "Tea?"

"Not yet." She sits in the chair with the good back and finds that even sitting is work. He brings the lemon mug, sets it left of the sink, then moves it to the table. He does not hover.

Ruth knocks once, looks, reads the colour in Joy's face. "Panadol?"

"Yes."

Ruth leaves and returns with a strip and a small container of soup that says *heat me on a piece of tape*. "Ring if worse," she says and goes.

He finds the folder without being told. Opens to *Numbers*. Leaves it open. He does not call anyone. He heats the soup slow, checks it once, twice, stops before boiling. He sets it down with a spoon.

"Later," she says. He leaves it.

Midday. She sleeps. He steps outside, shuts the door, opens the safe, tests the code, closes it, re-enters. Ten seconds. Habit cements.

He takes the bins to the kerb and brings them back because he is a day early. He writes *Thursday* on his envelope and underlines it once.

He eats bread and cheese. He rinses the knife and leaves it point up. He wipes the bench and misses a ring; sees it; wipes again.

Afternoon, he walks to the chemist with the envelope in his pocket.

"Panadol," he says, and the pharmacist passes a box with the adult dose printed large.

He pays. He keeps the receipt. At home he sets the tablets by the water glass. "Two," he says.

She takes them. She sleeps again. There are no dreams. There is no expansion.

He reads the paper without turning a page and feels no need to pretend. He moves the chair he fixed a hand's width to make room for the heater and does not set it too close. He puts a towel on the rail to dry and does not fold it.

Near four Ruth knocks once and leaves a note: *I'll do bins if needed — R.* He slides it into the folder at the front, under *If I'm not here.*

She wakes, steadier. "Soup," she says.

He heats it again, slow. Brings it. Stays long enough to see the spoon move twice, then leaves. *Her rage has shrunken to a whiff.*

Evening he eats toast; she eats the rest of the soup. He takes two tablets from the dish and puts them back because they are not his. He sets his own dish down and lifts each pill. *Do not name them one by one.* He takes them in silence.

Before bed he writes *bins — Thursday* on the calendar in small letters. He puts the pen back parallel to the edge.

In the dark she coughs. He says, "All right?"

"All right," she says.

The folder sits on the sideboard. The safe is shut. The door is on latch. The list on the envelope goes in the bin. She sinks into a pitch black darkness.

36

Hall, Solo

Morning's pale. She's better but not sure. "Not today," she says to the hall.

He nods, ties his laces. *He must have found his shoes by himself.*

"Map?" she asks.

"In the folder," he says. He doesn't take it. He pockets his wallet, phone, the small square. He leaves the keys in the bowl. Coat, hat. "Ten," he says.

She does not walk him to the door. The latch clicks.

Quiet. She sits in the chair with the good back. She makes tea and leaves it to cool. *Silence.*

At the hall: paint tins propping the door; wet coats; the tub of mixed screws. Mara's nod. "Lamps again. A pram with a wheel that stutters. Three handles for the op shop drawers."

He takes the bench at the end. Dale hasn't come yet. Ed lifts a toaster. The boy brings the pram. "Won't track," he says. Art tips it, spins the wheel, finds the grit under the cap. He explains at length. The boy listens, yawns behind his hand.

Pin out, grit out, a flick of oil, pin in. He rolls it across the boards. True.

"Thanks," the boy says.

"Handle?" Art asks, and the boy brings one. Art explains. The boy yawns behind his hand. Art drills first. Screw goes in without protest. He shows the boy the entry with the grain. "Next time," he says.

The boy nods.

Dale arrives late, rain on his shoulders. Lifts two fingers. "Traffic," he says to the floor.

Ed measures the shelf twice and cuts once.

At eleven-forty-five Mara claps once. "Pack up."

He wipes the bench with his palm and then the cloth. He puts a lone brass screw in the small pocket on the bag. Outside, he takes the short way home not using the map. At the door he uses the key from the safe because the habit is still warm. "Back," he says.

"Good?" she asks.

"Busy," he says and sets the bag by the sideboard, square on top, taps it once. He brings two mugs to the table without looking for coasters. She does not say: "Coasters".

She eats a bit of toast. He eats the other half. He puts the plate in the rack the right way up and leaves it near enough straight. After lunch he takes the pram wheel cap from his pocket—a spare he didn't need to keep—and leaves it on the sideboard like a reminder.

She writes three lines:

Hall without me.

Pram wheel true.

Square home, no map.

In the late afternoon Dale knocks with a single word: "Wednesday?"

"Two," Art says.

Dale points his chin at the safe. "Sensible," he says, and goes.

In the evening he moves the chair a hand's width back. Before bed he stands at the door and checks the latch with two fingers, the old carpenter's test. *Why?*

"Tomorrow," he says.

Tomorrow what?

She feels feverish still. Her blood seems to pulse inside of her. He lies beside her. *A stranger. Who is he?* She feels cold.

37

The Visit

Thursday, just after ten. A knock that is not Ruth's. The lay visitor in the blue dress stands on the step with a folder and a smile. "Short visit," she says. "Fifteen."

"Come in," Joy says.

Art is at the table with the easy crossword turned to the back. He stands, then sits again.

"I'm Helen," the woman says. "From church."

"Joy," Joy says, though Helen knows.

"Art."

"Lovely to meet you properly," Helen says to the room. She takes the chair that faces both of them making a triangle.

"How are we travelling?" she asks.

"Local," Art says.

"Good radius," Helen says.

She opens the folder. "I'm here to see if anything practical would be useful," she says. "Not to sign you up for anything. I can leave cards and you can ignore them."

Joy nods.

"Transport sometimes helps," Helen says. "Short notice lifts. Hospital runs. We've got three drivers who don't mind daylight jobs."

"Daylight," Art repeats.

"Or a meal," Helen adds. "Not a roster. Just a drop when someone's cooked extra."

"No meals," Joy says. "We manage."

"Fine," Helen says. She pens a small tick, then keeps the pen still.

"Cards on Thursdays," Art says.

"Lovely," Helen says. "Where?"

"Dale's or Len's."

"Good men," Helen says.

Joy brings the folder from the sideboard and sets it on the table. She opens the first sleeve. "Numbers are here," she says. "If we need you, we'll call. If something happens, everything is in here."

Helen glances once. "Excellent."

Art taps the map with one finger. "Left after the oval," he says. "Back way."

Today he's bad, real bad.

"Back ways are my favourite," Helen says.

Art smiles. He closes the folder.

Helen looks at the side wall through the window. "Is that a key safe?"

"Yes," Joy says.

"Good placement," Helen says. "Under the eave."

"We've told two," Joy says.

"Enough," Helen says. She puts a business card on the table and slides it two inches towards them. "My mobile. The office. If I don't answer, someone will."

"We won't need meals," Joy says again.

"Noted," Helen says. "What about sitting? If you wanted to go to your thing—book group?—and you'd rather someone be here than not?"

"He doesn't need a sitter," Joy says. *Yet.*

"I don't need a sitter," Art says, at the same time.

"Good," Helen says. "Then I'll mark us as available if asked and not as anything else." She turns one page. "Any paperwork you want to discuss? Advance care, contacts, legal next of kin. Some people like to make sure their name is spelled right in the office list."

"We've got the folder," Joy says. "We're not on your books."

"Fair," Helen says. "Spelling will have to fend for itself." She closes her folder. "Two minutes more and I'm done," she says. "We've a men's morning on Fridays at the hall, but I heard you've got Tuesdays at the hall."

"Tools Tuesday," Art says.

"Perfect." She stands. "I won't bother you with follow-ups. If you need a driver, say 'driver'. If you need a visit, say 'visit'."

"Thank you," Joy says.

Helen looks at the gate through the glass. "I'll see you at church when you feel like it," she says. "Or I won't." She leaves without fuss. The door shuts. The room returns to itself.

Art says, "Good radius," as if trying the word.

"Useful word," Joy says. *What a conversation!*

He opens the folder and moves the business card into the front sleeve behind *If I'm not here.* He closes the folder and taps it once with two fingers. There.

She keeps her face very still. This is not easy.

After lunch, he walks alone to the corner and back. On return he pauses at the side wall, opens the safe, shuts it, opens it again, not counting out loud. He comes inside and doesn't report.

Ruth knocks later, leaning in with a loaf. "Blue dress?" she asks.

"Yes."

"Harmless," Ruth says. "Useful when asked."

"Driver, maybe," Joy says, "sometimes."

"Let someone fuss," Ruth says. "It's good for them."

"Maybe," Joy says. *Maybe?*

Ruth's eyes go to the folder on the sideboard. "Still sitting there," she says.

"It lives in the sideboard," Joy says. But we're still looking at it.

Afternoon, the hall calls. Mara. "The boy wants to learn to plane properly," she says. "We can do Saturday if Tuesday's full."

"Tuesday," Art says. "Slow is fine."

"Slow it is," Mara says, and hangs up.

Slow is fine. What does that mean? I used to understand him. I don't anymore.

He takes the small plane from the shed and brings it inside. Sets it on the bench, sole down. He checks the iron with his thumbnail and turns the adjuster a touch.

Joy writes three lines:

Helen, fifteen, no kettle.

Driver only if asked.

Plane on the bench, iron set fine.

Evening. He eats, rinses, sets the plate in the rack. She leaves it. Before bed he stands at the door and checks the latch by feel. He says nothing. She says nothing back.

In the dark he says, after a minute, "We're not on a roster."

"No," she says.

"Good," he says.

She closes her eyes. Stars and galaxies pass her with dazzling speed. Her legs are behind her. She's flying, arms wide. She can see the red shoes when she looks back under her arm. She's everywhere at once. She wakes. Sits up, writes something in her notebook with the light off.

38

Shavings

Tuesday. Cold that makes metal stick. When she looks at her notebook, it reads: *Everywhere at once. Blind writing.*

The day begins. *Poop travelling through a body. Inch by inch.* Square in the bag. Plane wrapped in an old tea towel.

The hall door is propped with paint tins. Mara nods them in. "The bench is yours," she says. The boy is already there, hands in pockets, trying not to look keen.

"Knife line," Art says. He gives the boy the knife and embarks on a lengthy explanation. The boy yawns behind his hand.

"Light. Twice."

The boy scores along the grain, shallow.

Art nods. "Again."

The third pass is quieter. He sets the plane on the timber and checks the iron with his thumbnail. A hair of light. "Fine," he says.

The boy watches his hands. "Weight front," Art says. "Then back. Don't rock."

The first stroke chatters.

He steps aside and lets the boy try. Skitter.

He takes the plane, sets it down, starts over. "Stand here. Feet like this."

The next pass sings. A curl lifts, thin as onion skin. "Listen," Art says.

The boy listens.

Dale arrives with a drawer that bites. He glances across, sees the lesson, doesn't interrupt.

Ed brings a toaster that smells wrong and occupies himself with screws.

"Against the grain?" the boy asks.

"Don't," Art says. "Turn the wood." He flips the piece, shows the change in shine. Explains.

The boy nods. They work. Stroke, set, stroke. Shavings build against the vice like pale drift. Art brushes them aside with the back of his hand.

The boy copies the gesture.

"Your turn again," Art says.

The boy planes a clean ribbon, holds it up to the light. He grins.

Art allows himself half a smile. "The dnd grain will tear. Stop before it occurs. Pare with the chisel." *Full sentences!*

He shows the angle, the quiet pressure.

The boy breathes shallow and gets it near enough.

Art does not correct the last millimetre.

Mara passes with rags. "Looks like teaching," she says.

"Slow," Art answers.

"Slow is best," Mara says, and moves on. At eleven forty-five she claps once. "Pack."

The boy gathers shavings with both hands and tips them into the bin. "Thanks," he says. He wipes the plane with a clean rag without being told and sets it sole down.

Art nods.

Outside, Joy waits under the awning with two paper cups. "Home?" she asks.

"Home," he says. He carries the plane, wrapped in its tea towel.

At the kitchen table he lays the tea towel out and opens it like a parcel. He checks the iron once more, backs it off a fraction, oils the sole with a fingertip, re-wraps. He sets the plane on the sideboard beside the folder and the screws tin.

She writes three lines:

Knife line, twice.

Shaving held to light.

Slow on purpose.

In the afternoon he goes to the shed and planes—two strokes across a scrap, just sound—and stops. He sweeps the curls into his palm and puts them in the bin.

Dale knocks at two. "Oval?"

"Oval," Art says. The walk is cold and straight. At the gate Dale says: "Kid'll remember the knife, not the plane."

"Knives make you careful."

In the evening, he eats, rinses, sets the plate almost straight. She leaves it. Before bed, he lifts the tea towel once, checks the plane, lowers the cloth.

In bed she's back where the stars and planets rush past her with dizzying speed. She writes blind in her notebook again after she jolts.

39

Optometrist

She walks downstairs while looking in her notebook. *Who is the crazy one here?* It says. "Well, that's really useful," she says quietly to herself.

Reminder on the sideboard, not the fridge. She says, "Today."

Glasses," he says.

She fetches his shoes. One foot. The other foot. First pulling his socks up high. Tying his laces. Pulling the socks up again. She tries not to look.

The shop smells of lens cleaner and cardboard. Frames line the walls.

"Art?" the optometrist says. "I'm Mei."

"Art," he says.

Chart first. With glasses. Without. Letters. He gets most and leaves the last two unclaimed.

"Driving's daylight only," Mei says, reading the note from Malik. "We'll keep it that way."

He nods.

Field test. Puff of air. He blinks once. The machine hums and prints a small truth.

"Reading," Mei says, and holds up the card with paragraphs.

He takes her spare frame with the clip-ons and reads the first line, then the second.

"Stronger close work," she says. "Distance steady."

"For at the bench," he says.

She looks up. "Woodwork?"

"Plane," he says.

She chooses two frames that won't get in the way. "These will take a knock," she says. "Anti-glare for day."

He tries both. The heavier one sits where it should. He lifts his head, lowers it, checks the angle on himself in the mirror and then looks away.

"Show me your usual," Mei says.

He hands over the old pair.

She checks the screws, tightens one. "Keep these as spare," she says. "Label inside the case if you like."

"No label," he says.

"Then the case tells you," she says, and writes *SPARE* on the inside flap in pencil, small.

Joy sits with the invoice and pays. Pick-up in five days. She doesn't write it down. Mei does and tucks the slip into the case with *SPARE*.

On the way home he reads the street signs loud to himself. Left after the oval. Blue sign. Correct. At the house he puts the spare case on the sideboard beside the folder and the screws tin.

Five days. The shop bell again. Mei fits the new frames and waits while his eyes adjust.

"Better?" she asks.

He reads the small print on the cleaning cloth. "Microfibre," he says, pleased.

"Two rules," Mei says. "On your face or in the case. And don't wipe with your shirt."

He nods. "On my face," he says. "Or in the case."

At home he moves the fish magnet down one notch. He sets the cleaner on the sideboard where he won't drink it by accident. In the afternoon he planes a scrap with the new lenses on. He smiles to the wood.

She writes three lines:

Distance steady.

Close stronger.

On your face or in the case.

Evening, he reads the TV captions without leaning forward. He sets the glasses in the case when he is done. *He is in good boy mode.*

She lets the stars and planets wash over her. Again, there is that light. Warm and yellow and huge. *Am I having a near-death experience?* She decides to ask the counsellor who is as lonely as she is. *Two souls grasping at straws. Only he's younger. He doesn't know yet it only gets worse.*

40

The Fence

Alan at the gate with a glove in one hand and a post cap in the other. "Back fence leans," he says. "You've got the eye."

Art looks past him. Embarks on a lengthy explanation. Joy tries not to listen.

"Brace," he says.

"Can you—" Alan starts.

"Show you," Art says.

He even interrupts Alan.

They walk to Alan's, take the square, the saw, the tin with mixed screws—Graham's—and two lengths from the shed. The ground is wet. The post isn't rotten. The rails are tired.

"Knife line," Art says. He marks the brace ends shallow, twice, then gives Alan the knife. "Light."

Alan follows.

They set the first brace from post to lower rail.

"Hold," Art says.

Alan holds.

Art drills a pilot and then two more because timber splits. Screw bites.

"Second," Art says.

They flip the offcut, change the angle, mirror the first. The fence shifts a thumb's width back to where it used to be.

"Cap?" Alan asks, showing the plastic lid.

"Bin," Art says. He fits a timber cap with two short screws and a tap to settle.

Joy stands in their yard, within voice. Ruth watches from her side with a bin lid in her hand like a shield.

"Need a prop?" Alan asks.

"Pack it," Art says. He pares a shim from the old brace end with three quiet strokes.

The chisel breathes. The shim slides in and holds. "There."

They step back.

"Cost me?" Alan says, half-joking.

"Tea at our place," Art says.

Inside, two mugs, biscuits. They stand by the bench and drink. Alan's hands show small cuts. "Hall on Tuesday?" he asks.

"Tools," Art says.

"I'll bring a hinge," Alan says. "The back gate whines."

"It needs a spacer," Art says.

Alan nods.

When Alan goes, Art rinses the mugs and leaves them. He picks up the screw tin, takes out one brass, returns it, closes the lid.

Joy writes three lines:

Brace, not prop.

Shim from waste.

Plastic cap binned.

In the afternoon he walks alone, hands in pockets. He stops at the post and presses with two fingers, the test he trusts. It doesn't give.

Dale knocks at two. "Oval?"

"Oval," Art says. Dale points with his chin at the fence. "Sorted?"

"Brace," Art says.

They walk the long side of the oval because the short side is muddy. At the far corner Dale says, "Kid'll bring a hinge. Says you like spacers."

In the evening, Alan texts a photo of the fence. *Holds. Thanks.*

Art types: *Of course.* Sends.

Before bed he takes the small chisel from the shed and lays it on the sideboard beside the plane, sole down, iron covered. He checks the edge with a thumb. "Tomorrow," he says to no one, glad there is still work the world will let him do.

She swims towards the light. A warm glow envelopes her.

41

The Stone

Cold that makes breath show. He sets the small oil stone on the hall bench. The boy is there early, hands jammed in pockets.

"Not water," Art says. "Oil." He tips a coin of it on the stone and lets it find the pits. He embarks on a long slow explanation. The boy yawns behind his hand and nods.

The plane iron comes first. Art loosens the cap, slides the iron clear, holds it up so the light shows the nick that made it rasp. "There," he says. He lays the back flat, lets the stone do the work. No rocking.

"Count," he tells the boy.

The boy whispers numbers.

"Flip," Art says. "Now the bevel. Don't climb."

The boy lifts his elbows.

Art taps one down with two fingers. "Here," he says, and sets the angle by feel.

The iron strokes. Grey gathers in the oil. A burr arrives.

"Feel it," Art says.

The boy feels.

"Strop," Art says, and gives him the scrap of leather he has carried in his bag. "Back first. Then bevel."

The boy pulls, slow. The edge brightens.

"Plane sole?" the boy asks.

"Don't," Art says. "Stone is for edges. Wax for soles."

The boy nods.

Dale sets a drawer on the next bench and glances across. "You sharpening the world?" he says.

"Just this bit," Art says.

Ed, who trusts plugs more than edges, brings a box of kettles. He sorts, fails one with a tick, passes two, sets one aside for a new plug.

The chisel now. Art cradles it. "Don't chase perfect," he says. "Chase straight."

"Same angle?" the boy asks.

"Near," Art says. He sets it on the stone. "Listen."

They both listen.

The scrape changes.

The boy notices.

That is the lesson.

"Your turn," Art says. He does not correct the first pass. He corrects the second with a tap. The third finds its line.

"Burr," the boy says.

"Strop," Art says.

The boy pulls, cleaner. The edge catches the light.

"Test," Art says, and hands him a length of pine.

The boy pares. A fat curl pushes then thins, then clears. "End grain?" he asks.

"Not today," Art says.

Mara brings rags. At eleven forty-five she claps once.

The boy wipes the stone with a paper towel and hands it back with two hands. He wraps the plane iron in the tea towel with care.

"Thanks," he says.

"Bring your own next time," Art says.

The boy nods.

Outside, the air bites. Joy stands under the awning with a cup. "Home," she says.

"Home," he says, and takes the cup and drinks it near the door.

At the table he opens the tea towel, lays out the iron and the chisel. He wipes both with a clean rag, light oil, not too much. He closes the oil, sets it on the sideboard with the cap down.

She writes three lines:

Burr arrived like a word.

Don't chase perfect.

Strop on leather, back first.

He goes to the shed and finds a scrap of hardwood. He planes once. The shavings lift like ribbon. He sets the chisel on the end grain and stops himself. "Tomorrow," he says.

Dale knocks at two. "Oval?""Oval," Art says. They take the long side again. At the far corner Dale says, "Kid asked about stones." "Good," Art says.

"The boy asked for links," Dale says.

"Tell him the library," Art says. "And his hands."

After, Ruth leans in with a bag of mandarins. "It's cold," she says.

"Stone," he says. He puts one mandarin on the window ledge where the sun finds it and keeps the others where fruit goes. He peels the one on the ledge later, clean long spiral, sets the peel in the sink.

Evening is quiet. He eats with the even chew that drives her nuts, sets the plate near straight, leaves it. He opens the folder to slide a small card in—*Oil stone:* —then closes it.

Before bed he looks at the chisel once again. He wraps it again and places it beside the plane, sole down, iron clean.

She turns out the light.

The house needs nothing sharpened, nothing oiled. He stands in the middle of the room, seemingly lost, then turns off the light on her.

She now writes words in her notebook blindly. She may use them later. She is an author after all.

42

End Grain

Her notebook says: *Light. Warmth.* In huge uneven letters. Cold with sun. He unwraps the plane and the chisel and lays them on the table. "Hall," he says.

"Yes," she says.

The boy is there early, his hair damp.

"End grain," Art says and embarks on a long explanation. The boy yawns behind his hand.

Art clamps a short block upright. "Knife first."

The boy scores the top light, twice.

Art sets the chisel just inside the line. "Pare to it. Don't climb."

Quiet pressure. A curl that isn't a curl, more a dust, lifts and shows clean fibres.

"Your turn," Art says.

The first pass skitters. He taps the handle with two fingers. "Here."

The boy drops his elbow. The edge begins to listen. Two more passes. "Back bevel?" the boy asks.

"No."

They flip the block and repeat. The knife line catches the light and gives it back. The boy stops a hair early. Art does not rescue. "Good enough is better than torn," he says.

Dale lifts another drawer onto the next bench.

Ed plugs a lamp into the board with the big red switch.

"Chamfer," Art says, and tilts the plane for the boy. Two passes to knock the edge, one to agree with the second. "Stop before the corner. Come from the other side. Meet without blowing out."

"Strop," Art says. The leather darkens where the iron has passed. The edge brightens.

"Test," Art says, and points at the end grain.

The boy pares.

Mara brings rags. "Looks like patience," she says.

"Boredom with style," Art says. The boy laughs.

At eleven forty-five the clap. They pack. Outside, under the awning, Joy has one cup. "Home?"

"Home," he says.

At the table he wipes the irons, backs the screws a fraction, lays the plane sole down, the chisel face up. He sets the oil where it lives and he won't drink it by accident.

She writes three lines:

Don't collect tricks.

End grain without tear.

Meet the corners.

After lunch he takes the short block to the shed and sets it on the sill.

Dale knocks at two. "Oval?"

"Oval," Art says.

They walk the long side because the short side is still puddled. At the far corner Dale says: "Kid'll be dangerous with sharp things."

"Dangerous is fine," Art says. "Careful is better."

Back home, Alan leans over the fence. "Back gate cries," he says. "Brought the hinge."

"Spacer," Art says, already reaching for the tin. They walk to Alan's back gate. They set it with two screws and a tap. The gate stops complaining.

Evening, he puts the chisel and plane back in their places and taps the tea towel once as he covers them. He rinses a glass and leaves it near enough straight. She leaves it.

Before bed he says, to the dark: "Corners met."

"They did," she says. *What are we talking about?* She departs. The light isn't coming closer, no matter how far and fast she flies, it stays at a distance. Then she is in a boat. Rowing, her back toward a dark sea. She sees their house on the shore. It looks like it's made of Lego. It starts crumbling. She doesn't care. She keeps rowing. She hears the oars hitting the water. Splash, splash, splash. Her body knows no age. She is capable of anything. The house disappears. She is alone at sea. Unafraid. Alone is good. She'll be fine when he dies.

43

The Service

Her notebook's blind page reads: *Splash. Splash. Splash.*

Ruth points with her chin at the Ute. "Listen," she says. A belt squeals once, stops.

"Book it," Joy says.

He takes the folder, finds a number, keys it in his phone, rings the local: *Mick's Auto — Service & Tyres.*

"Eight-thirty, Thursday," Mick says. "Drop and walk. Couple of hours."

"Daylight," Art says.

"Plenty," Mick says.

Thursday is bright. He puts the licence card in his wallet and the glasses on his face.

At the counter, Mick's hands are clean in the way mechanics manage for the first minute of the day. "How's she running?"

"Short runs," Art says. "Daylight. Belt squeals cold."

"Seen worse," Mick says. "Oil, filter, coolant, belt. Wipers if they chatter."

"Chatter," Art says.

"Done," Mick says.

Joy leaves her number; then crosses it out and writes his.

"We'll walk," Art says.

They take the path by the oval. He names parts out loud once—belt, idler, plug—and then stops. At Ruth's he lifts a hand. She lifts hers back.

At ten-fifteen the phone rings. He answers. "Mick," the voice says. "Tyres are legal, close. Battery fine. Belt was glazed. Replaced. Coolant low—topped. Wipers new. Front left indicator intermittent. Earth loose—cleaned and refit."

"Good," Art says. "Pay now or later?"

"Later," Mick says. "Before four if you want daylight."

"Before four," Art says. He hangs up, sets the phone down, doesn't recount anything. She doesn't ask. She's heard everything anyway.

Later, he takes the old wipers from the boot where Mick left them and sets them on the bench like a souvenir. "Chattered," he says, testing the past tense.

He puts on his coat. "Walk," he says.

She nods.

They go the back way.

At the counter, Mick slides the invoice across. Items in caps, numbers aligned. "Card?"

Art presents it the right way first time. The machine chirps. "All good," the screen says.

"Keep the old belt?" Mick asks, half-teasing.

"Bin," Art says. "Souvenirs are trip hazards."

Mick grins. "Fair." He taps the indicator lens with a knuckle. " Shouldn't sulk now."

"Good," Art says.

They drive home the short way. He parks straight and too carefully. He checks the wiper action. Smooth. He checks the indicator once. Blink, blink, even. He closes the ute gently.

Inside, he lays the invoice in the folder sleeve behind *Car*.

Joy writes three lines:
Chattered past tense.
Earth cleaned.
Souvenirs are trip hazards.
Ruth knocks and leans. "Sorted?"
"Belt, wipers, earth," Art says.
"Take it round the block," she says to Joy.
"He will," Joy says.
After lunch he goes alone, a single orbit of the block. He returns in five minutes and sets the keys in the bowl. "Still smooth," he says.
"Good," she says.
He takes the old wipers to the bin and changes his mind at the lid. He wipes it with the tea towel and leaves it on the sideboard for now.
Dale knocks at two. "Oval?"
"Oval," Art says. "Belt's new."
"Good," Dale says, amused. They walk the long side. At the far corner Dale says, "Mick's a straight one."
"Earth," Art says.
Back home, Alan leans over the fence. "Got her seen to?"
"Belt, wipers, earth. Tyres later," Art says.
"Ring me when you do," Alan says. "I'll follow you in the second car."
Art nods.
Evening, Brendan texts: *Mechanic okay?*
When do they talk?
Art types: *Belt, wipers, earth.*
Good stuff, Brendan replies.
Before bed, Art takes the wiper from the sideboard and slides it into the bag with the square and the plane, wrapped in the old tea towel. He sets the bag by the door and taps it once. *God help us!*

She adds one more line in the notebook: *Invoice in sleeve, rule in head. Broken window wiper.* Closes it.

The house hums. Winter holds. The left-after-the-oval still works. The keys are in the bowl.

She thinks about the lonely counsellor and what he said: "Your mind makes fantasies when the days are boring. People in prison know this." *Fantasies.* The word sounds vulgar somehow. She thought she was having inspiration. For a book. *What book?* She falls into her young body.

44

The Tyres

Monday's clear. He stands at the ute and presses a thumbnail into the front left. "Legal, close," he says.

"Today," she says.

"Just be be safe."

He rings Mick's Tyres, same sign, different side of the yard. "Two fronts," Mick says. "Standard. Be here by eleven. Forty minutes. Bring the card."

Joy feels a surge of love for him. *He's doing things.*

Alan leans over the fence at ten-thirty with his car keys already in his hand. "Follow, not lead," he says.

"Local," Art says. Mick's close enough."

They go in a neat line: ute first, Alan behind, Joy beside him.

At the bay, Mick points a tread gauge into the grooves and shows the small teeth. "Just on the marker," he says. "Backs can wait. You want quiet, rain-friendly. Not fancy."

"Not fancy," Art repeats.

"Rotation after," Mick says. He chalks a white X on the left rear.

They sit on plastic chairs. A TV in the corner shows a cooking show without sound. Joy opens her book and doesn't read it. Alan checks something on his phone and pockets it again.

Mick lifts a tyre and shows the sidewall. "No bulges," he says, pleased. "Balanced then aligned. Steering'll stop correcting itself."

"Good," Art says.

"Coffee across the road," Mick adds, but they stay.

Forty minutes is forty-five. The alignment board glows green. The car lowers. Mick wipes his hands on a rag. "Card?"

Art presents it the right way first time. The machine chirps. "All good," the screen writes.

"Keep the old?" Mick asks, half out of habit.

"Bin," Art says. "Trip hazards."

Mick grins. "You're a man after my own back." He taps the tread with a knuckle. "Run them in easy for a day. No heroics in the wet."

"No heroics," Art says.

Alan pulls out behind them and keeps a gap. On the straight before the oval he flashes his lights once and peels off. Art waves. Hands back on the wheel quickly, daylight, local.

Just in case Alan.

Home, he parks straight and rechecks the new tread. He puts the invoice in the folder behind *Car.*

Lunch is toast. "Steering holds," he says to the room. "Doesn't seek."

Orations for when he has an audience, one-liners for me.

"Good," she says.

After, he takes the old pressure gauge from the drawer and checks all four. He adds air to the rears only, slow puffs. Cap on, cap on, cap on, cap on.

Ruth knocks once. "New shoes?" she says from the step.

"Fronts," he says.

"Run them in," she says.

"Easy," he says.

At two, Dale knocks with one word: "Oval?"

"Oval," Art says. They walk. On the far side Dale says, "Feels different?"

"Holds," Art says.

"Good," Dale says.

Back home he writes *Tyres—fronts* on a small card, the tidy caps he taught, and slides it behind the invoice so only the top edge shows. He sets the gauge beside the screws tin and leaves it there till evening, then returns it to the drawer.

She writes three lines:

Legal, now honest.

No heroics.

Steering stops correcting itself.

Near dusk he takes the ute round the block once, brakes gentle at the corner, hands steady. He returns in five minutes, sets the keys in the bowl.

"Smooth," he says.

"Good," she says.

He stands at the door and tests the latch with two fingers.

Evening comes with him turning the light off on her. In the living room this time.

So she is "grieving" and she is "bored". Instead of "inspired" and "setting boundaries". She writes the words in the dark on her blind page. She falls into her younger body and runs, runs. She arrives at a rocky outcrop. She jumps lightly from rock to rock. In the little rock pools are universes so beautiful and attractive that one loses oneself in them. She tries not to look. But one pulls her in. A kaleidoscope of colourful sea plants and fish shooting this way and that way. She loses herself like someone on hard drugs. It washes over her like hot tar. She does not know any longer who she is.

45

Late

Her blind page says: *Who am I?*

Book group runs over. Rain. The lonely therapist. She texts *late* and puts the phone back.

At home he reads the word, nods to no one, and sets the folder on the bench: If I'm not here—Ruth. Malik. He doesn't need either. He makes toast. He eats it standing. He rinses the knife and turns it the right way in the rack. He sets a glass near enough straight.

A knock. Courier in a high-vis jacket with SIGNATURE RE-QUIRED on the satchel.

"Joy?"

"Here," Art says.

"Name?"

"Art." He signs his own, steady. The man hands over a small parcel with the optometrist's return address. Frames cloth, cleaner, a case. He puts it on the sideboard with the other stuff.

Another knock, quick. Alan. "Hinge for the side gate? Got the right size this time."

"Tomorrow," Art says. "Rain."

"Tomorrow," Alan agrees.

Art walks to the hall and opens the sideboard. He puts the folder there. He taps it. He closes the door.

At four, the light thins. He switches on two lamps. He writes a line on the small card in his wallet—*Ruth bins—Thu*—and then crosses it out because he already wrote it on the calendar yesterday. He smiles at having found himself ahead.

The rain gives up. Wind takes over, low. The side wall safe is dry. He steps out, opens it, shuts it, opens; the numbers in his mouth. He leaves it shut and comes back in.

Brendan texts: *You two okay?*

Art types: *Rain. Your mother late*. Sends.

He folds the tea towel over the chair he fixed and sits. He thinks about the square in the hall. He stands, checks the bag by the door, taps it once. He takes the tool oil from the sideboard and touches the door hinges with a dot each. He wipes the excess with the corner of the towel and leaves no gloss.

Footsteps outside. The key turns. She steps in, damp.

"Late, sorry", she says.

Parcel on the sideboard, glass near straight, two lamps on. "All right," she says to the house.

"Courier came," he says. "Frames and cloth."

"Good." She takes off her coat and hangs it on the peg.

They stand at the kitchen bench with two mugs. "Alan's tomorrow," he says. "Hinge side gate. If the weather will allow it."

She opens the cupboard and closes it again.

"Thanks," she says, though there's nothing to thank him for.

He lifts a hand the way men do. "All right," he says.

Evening is simple. They eat a simple meal. He chews. He rinses. The parcel sits with the screws tin and the plane, each given a square of wood.

Before bed he sets his glasses in the case—on your face or in the case—and turns the hall light off while she's climbing the stairs. Rage surges through her and leaves again.

The rain doesn't return. Winter ends here without announcement. She falls into a rock pool with her younger body. Her red shoes stand at its shore on the rocks.

46

Observation

S he's written *rage* on the blind page in her notebook. And *house-wife*. She remembers the counsellor had called her that. House-wife. *I am an author.* It's a warm morning that smells like wet dirt.

He stands slow, sits again. Heat at the temples.

"Malik" she says.

"Oh."

She fetches his shoes because he does not move. Sets them by his feet. He fishes for them with his feet. She tries not to look. Sock one up. Chin to the ceiling. Sock two up. Shoe one one, shoe two on. Sock one up. Sock two up. Chin at the ceiling. Tie shoe one. Tie shoe two. The socks. *Again.*

Malik's room at nine forty-five. Pulse is quick. Temperature is up. Urine strip. "UTI," he says. "Better observe than guess. Short stay in bed here."

Triage smells of antiseptic and windows that don't open. He sits. She stands. Paperwork does the talking.

"Allergy?"

"No."

"Next of kin?"

"Here."

"Falls?"

"Not lately."

The nurse writes.

She waits. He sways on his feet.

A bed behind a curtain. Fluids up. Antibiotics in. A doctor whose name slides off the badge says the word *infection*. "Overnight if fever lingers. Likely home by evening if it breaks."

He dozes. He doesn't snore. She sits. She doesn't read or write. Her fingers are in her lap. *Old hands*. She texts Dale.

Dale texts: *Need anything*.

She replies *No*.

Brendan writes *Should I come*.

She types *We're covered*.

Ruth appears with a sandwich. "Better than hospital tucker," she says to the room, as if food is the spine of a day.

"Thanks." says Joy. "You're a lifesaver, as usual."

Afternoon thins. The fever lifts the way fog does. He wakes, asks the time, does not repeat the question. The cannula tape itches; but he doesn't pick it, just says it. A physio with a ponytail checks his sit-to-stand. She says: "Short steps, no rushing."

At four, the doctor returns with the quiet permission voice. "Numbers look better. Oral antibiotics at home. See your GP next week."

Discharge is a small packet and a long form.

She signs.

He signs.

The nurse removes the cannula and hides the cotton ball under tape.

Ruth appears as if she had been standing just outside the door. "Ready?" she says.

He nods.

They go.

Daylight is still.

He does not realise Joy is going to the counsellor. She's never told him about the counsellor. *Or have I?*

Home by five. She lays the packet of pills on the table. She writes *with food* on the box and sets it beside the glass. He eats soup because soup is what you eat after hospitals. He swallows the first tablet without looking at it.

She fetches his folder and slides the discharge summary into a sleeve behind Malik.

Dale knocks once, head in. "Yum," he says when he sees the soup. "Wednesday still two?"

"Two," Art says.

"Okay," Dale says, and leaves them to it.

In the evening he rinses his bowl and sets it down. She leaves it. He walks to the side of the house. The key safe is dry. His map is back in the cupboard. He opens the door and taps it once. Before bed she circles *GP — Tues* on the calendar. He taps the calendat once with two fingers on the way past. "All right," he says.

"All right," she says.

Spring sits on the sill with the lemons. The house is lukewarm. He turns the light off in the kitchen with her in it. She is used to this now. She climbs the stairs well after he does. Women are not allowed anger or rage or other negative emotions, the lonely counsellor had said. Well, I have plenty. *Rage. Anger. Disgust. Not only at him. Well. Mainly at him.*

47

Review

Tuesday. Her blind page says: *Rage. Anger. Disgust.*

On the calendar, she circles *GP — 10:10.*

She brings the shoes. He pulls up his socks. Feet find the shoes. It takes forever. He pulls his socks up again. Ties his laces. *God help us.*

Reception knows their faces. "Take a seat."

The TV is off. Dr Malik opens the door himself. "Come in." He sits facing Art first. "How are you travelling?"

"Good," Art says.

"Any fever since?"

"No."

"Dizzy?"

"No."

"Eating?"

"Soup. Toast. Tomatoes. Cheese."

"Fine," Malik says. He reads the discharge summary out loud. "Bug's sensitive to what you're on. Finish the course. With food."

Art nods.

Vitals. Pulse steady. Pressure steady. Temperature okay. Malik taps the numbers into the record.

"Quick screen," he says. "Apple, table, penny?"

Apple," Art says. "Table." Beat. "Penny."

Malik's says: "Good."

"Driving," Joy says, keeping her voice thin so it doesn't take up the room. "Daylight and local only, remains unchanged?"

"Unchanged," Malik says. "Illness can wobble cognition for a week or two—don't test yourself for sport. Short runs. Daylight. No new routes. If you feel off, pull over and call." He looks at Art, not her. "You know the drill."

"I do," Art says.

"Urine check next week," Malik adds. "Nurse will give you the bottle. Drop in Monday. If it shows clear, we call; if not, we adjust." He prints the label. *Why do people not speak in sentences? Have they ever? Or am I noticing it only now? Texting is not sentences either. The only sentences I read are on flyers and in books and they live in my head.*

Malik turns the screen a degree. "Medications: continue as is. The antibiotic finishes Saturday. We'll keep the sleep tablet where it is."

Art nods once. "Simple."

"Good word," Malik says. "Simple keeps people out of here."

He looks at Joy last. "Any falls?"

"No."

"Any new wandering?"

"No," she says, and adds, "Wrong gate once. Fixed it with paint and a rosemary plant."

Malik nods. "Excellent." He signs, stamps, slides two slips across, both facing Art. "Specimen bottle. And the nurse line if you need it."

Art pockets both.

"Questions?" Malik asks.

"The hall," Art says. "On Tuesday."

"Keep it," Malik says. "Halls have fewer infections than hospitals. Better jokes too."

They leave. The bottle rattles in Art's pocket. *What else is in his pocket?*

In the car he puts it on the backseat and touches it with two fingers.

Home, she places the antibiotic box on the table, writes *Sat finishes* in tidy caps.

He takes one with food. The new slips find a sleeve behind Malik.

Ruth knocks. "All right?"

"All right," Joy says.

"I'll bring more soup later," Ruth says.

He walks to the gate and back. He stands at the side wall and opens the safe, shuts it, opens it again.

After lunch the phone pings. Brendan: *You two okay?*

Art types: *GP good. Bottle Monday.* Sends.

Proud of you Dad, Brendan replies.

He gets the mower out and doesn't start it. He looks at the grass, decides *future*, puts the mower back. He oils the catch on the shed door with a dot.

She sits at the table and writes three lines:

Finish Saturday.

Bottle Monday.

Simple keeps people out of here.

He takes the ute round the block once at three, daylight, local, the same turn. Keys back in the bowl.

Dale knocks at four. "Two tomorrow?"

"Two," Art says.

"Okay," Dale says.

"It sits," Art says. *It sits? Really?*

In the evening he eats, rinses, sets the plate near enough straight. She leaves it. The antibiotic box stands next to the glass. He swallows without complaint. Then the other pills. It takes forever. She looks at her hands.

Before bed she moves the fish magnet one notch down so the bottle reminder sits where a hand finds it first. He taps the sideboard once. "Monday," he says.

"Monday," she echoes.

Spring air comes in on the latch, mild. The plan is only: finish, test. He can do that. He turns off the light.

She sits in the darkness. Listening to the house. She is on top of things, as usual. But there is a new-ish feeling stuck in her. *Fear.* It is as if she is falling and filled up with adrenaline. It is as if she can die at any time. Hit the ground. When a plug is pulled or a string breaks. *Well, isn't that the reality? Always?*

48

Paperwork

The blind page in her notebook says: *Anxiety.* She's never used that word before. She's heard it, but never connected it to herself.

It's warm enough to open the window. She lifts the folder onto the table and sets a pen beside it. "Today," she says.

"Today," he answers. A jolt of fear passes through her. It makes her head go up and down slightly, as if she nods.

She lays out four thin piles: *Contacts, Money, Health, Preferences.*

Contacts first. She prints in tidy caps: Ruth (neighbour), Dale (friend), Alan (fence), Brendon (son) each with numbers. She adds *Mara — Hall* for someone who answers phones. He reads, nods once at each.

Money. One page: bank, pension, the name of the super fund. Balances. No passwords on paper. A single line: *statements live in top drawer.* He watches, says nothing, approves with quiet.

Health. She opens the Justice website on the laptop, prints the Medical Treatment Decision Maker form and the Advance Care Directive. Paper curls as it cools. She stacks it flat with a book.

"Who?" she asks.

"You," he says.

"Brendan as back-up?"

He nods. "Local first." He takes the pen and writes Brendan's number slow.

She prints the Enduring Power of Attorney information sheet, not the form. "Solicitor for this," she says. He nods.

Preferences. She writes in small, factual lines on a clean page:

Short service.

Cremation.

No speeches.

Music if needed: the hymn with anchor in the line.

Let Dale choose a photo if he wants. If he doesn't, none.

He reads it once. "True," he says.

True? Really?

She turns to her set. "You choose," she says.

"Ruth," he says. "Then Brendan." He taps the line where Brendan's name will go. She writes both. She adds a card: *Keys, folder, side wall safe.* He touches the words with two fingers.

Witnessing. She circles *JP at library* on the calendar for next week, small. "Not today," she says. "We'll do it properly."

"Book?" he asks.

"I will," she says, and types the email to the desk with the rubber bell: two appointments, ten minutes each, forms to witness. Thursday 11:30, the reply comes back before the kettle finishes.

She phones the community legal centre and asks for an appointment about powers. "Bring ID and the people you want," the voice says. She writes *ID* on a card and slides it into the sleeve with the forms.

He goes to the drawer and returns with two passport photos from years ago, the kind with bad lighting. "Proof," he says.

"Find the newer ones," she says, and puts them back in the drawer where they can't be used by mistake.

The funeral director's card from the church noticeboard goes in a sleeve without comment.

Organ donation is a box she doesn't tick on paper. "Registry handles that," she says. "Not for us to guess now." He nods, relieved.

She writes one last page headed *If He Is Out:*

Call Ruth.

Call Malik.

The folder sits on the sideboard.

Key safe: side wall. Code in mouths, not on paper.

He reads it and says, "If she is out," and she writes his mirror version under it, same lines.

At lunch he eats a sandwich and signs the MTDM page where a box says sign. He keeps his name inside the line. She leaves the witness spaces blank for Thursday. She signs her own copy after.

Ruth taps once, spots the stacks. She says: "Library JP?"

"Thursday."

"I'll come if you like," Ruth says. "Stand there and be a warm body while someone stamps things."

"Yes, come," Joy says.

Dale appears later with a hinge and a packet of screws. Sees the paperwork, doesn't ask. "Tomorrow," he says, and leaves the hinge on the bench.

She adds a card to the front sleeve: *Contacts in this order: Ruth →* *Malik → Dale → Brendan.* Not because Brendan is last; because he is far.

He takes the folder and stands by the sideboard. He moves the screws tin a hand's width, sets the folder down, returns the tin. He taps the folder once. "Lives here," he says.

"Lives there," she echoes.

Afternoon, she books the solicitor for the following Wednesday. "Bring ID," the receptionist says. "We'll keep it simple." She writes

Wed — wills/POA small on the calendar. She files the printed forms in sleeves: Health behind Contacts; POA/Wills behind Health; Preferences behind those.

In her notebook she writes three lines:

Appoint, don't announce.

Witness properly, not today.

Love written small.

In the evening he rinses, sets the plate near enough straight. She leaves it. Before bed, she shifts the fish magnet a notch so tomorrow's JP sits where a hand finds it first. He looks at the calendar, reads the small circles. He turns off the light in the kitchen. She moves to the living room. He turns off the lights in the living room with her in it. She sits in the dark. Spring runs along the fence. She walks up the stairs in the pitch dark.

Your needs are not met, the counsellor said. What about the counsellor's needs? Weren't they in the same boat? Still, it was good to go. *It gets me out of the house.*

In bed she runs with wild animals. Wolves, lions, a giraffe. They are weightless. So is she. They jump from rock to rock. Until a small rock pool overwhelms her. She travels through its tunnel towards the light. Always towards the light.

49

The Fixed Hours

In her notebook she finds the words: *He leaves darkness. Light = light.* She tries to remember what she meant when she wrote them. They seemed so meaningful then. So important. Now they mean nearly nothing.

The morning's bright enough to show dust. She does a round of dusting.

"Today," she says.

"Today," he answers.

I have not finished.

Ruth knocks once. Sees the words *book group* on the calendar under Tuesday. "Want me in the first week?"

"Tuesday," Joy says. "Light touch."

"Tea at mine if needed," Ruth says.

"He won't."

She messages Mara: *Hall—Tues 9–12? If Dale late, can you steer him to a bench?*

Mara replies: *Always.*

She texts Dale: *I'm out Tuesdays 9–12. Art still coming.*

Dale: *Good. I'll be there.*

She tells Brendan last, a single sentence: *I'll be unreachable Tues 9–12, Thurs 3–6.*

Proud of ye Mum, he sends back.

At a bit before nine Tuesday she puts her notebook in a bag. "Two hours," she says at the door.

"Two," he says. He has the bag with the square and the small plane. He taps the sideboard.

They part at the corner. He goes left to the hall. She goes right, past the bakery, to the bus stop. She does not check her phone.

At the hall Mara nods him to a bench that already has a task on it. The boy arrives on time. "End grain again?" he asks.

"Lines first," Art says. He explains. The boy yawns. They work. Dale arrives late, says nothing, takes a drawer, files the bite.

At eleven-forty-five the clap. He wipes the bench with his palm and then the cloth. He leaves the square in the bag and the bag by the door of the hall, ready for next Tuesday.

He is home at twelve-ten. She is twenty minutes after, notebook zipped. Book in hand.

"Good?" he asks.

"Good," she says.

On Thursday she lays a book on the table. "Three to six," she says.

"Book group again," he says.

Ruth knocks at two-forty and places two slices under foil on the bench. "Insurance," she say.

At three Joy walks to the library and sits in a ring of six people. She talks twice, softly. She listens to a man explain a sentence about wind as if he had invented air. She does not leave early. At four-fifty she writes a single phrase in her notebook: *Kindness without commentary.* She closes it.

At home he hasn't moved anything. He has eaten the first slice and left the second under foil. He didn't put it in the fridge, it is warm to the touch. He has set one glass near enough straight.

"How was your book?" he asks.

"Argued well," she says.

He nods.

She moves the fish magnet to show *JP — 11:30* for next week. He reads it and taps it once. "Ruth at ten," he says.

They trial the fixed hours again the next week. Tuesday he goes to the hall alone.

Dale is on time.

The boy arrives with his own oil stone, cheap, proud.

"Good," Art says. Even a bad stone teaches. They sharpen once, then work. Art embarks. The boy yawns.

Joy writes an hour on the bakery bench and spends the second sitting without writing, looking at the oval and the clouds. She calls that work.

Thursday she goes to book group and sits through a bad poem, which is a skill in itself. She tells the counsellor things are the same. She returns at six-twenty and finds a second slice untouched, warm to the touch.

"Saved it," he says. "For you."

"Thanks," she says, and doesn't eat it.

In her notebook she writes four lines:

Two hours are not a request.

Hall runs without me.

Book group argues well.

Lukewarm slices.

She laces her shoes and goes to the water alone and counts pelicans. Two. Then three. She returns. He is at the table with the easy page and the pencil he won't sharpen.

"Good?" he asks.

"Good," she says.

He taps the cupboard door once, where the map sits. "Map lives there," he says.

"Lives there," she answers.

Spring light finds the hall wall, then fades. He switches on the light and then leaves her in the dark. She sits and looks at her pale hands. She climbs the stairs well after him. She looks forward to the wild animals, the running, the rock pools. But they do not come. She has learned a new word today at the library. The man who explained. A *mansplainer. Mansplaining.* She smiles. She likes new words. They are brilliant. *I'm a mankeeper. He used to be a mansplainer. I thought it was the way to be. Listening. Nodding. Saying yes. Doing yes.* Now that the new words exist this seems old-fashioned. She is ready for new things. He is not.

50

Handover

Her blind page says: *Brutal.* She tries to remember why.

Tuesday's bright. Plane and square in the bag, oil stone left at home on purpose.

"The bench is yours," Mara says to the boy as they come in.

"Project?" Art asks.

The boy lifts a small drawer from a cheap bedside. Side catches. "Sticks."

"Show me," Art says.

The boy checks the grain with a thumb, finds the rise. Knife line, light, twice. He pares the end grain without tearing. He flips, meets the corners. He sets the plane for a whisper and knocks the edge once, then once from the other side. He smiles.

"Runners," Art says, tapping the carcass with authority.

The boy answers with a strip planed from a scrap, 2 mm proud, then trued. PVA, two pins. Clamp. He doesn't ask for the clamp; he takes it and leaves the last quarter turn for the wood.

Dale arrives with a gate latch and watches.

Ed fails a toaster and a kettle.

Mara drifts past and stays at the edge of the bench. "Looks like a plan," she says.

"Listen," Art says, and stands back.

The boy listens to the small things—the squeak gone where oil found its mark, the rasp of a too-dry runner, the hush when the drawer slides true for the first time. He pulls it out again and resists the urge to close too fast. "There," he says.

"Glue on your sleeve," Art says.

The boy wipes it with the rag. He sands once with a block. He blows dust the wrong way, catches himself, and moves.

"Square?" Dale asks, chin at the tool.

"His," Art says.

"Next time." He runs a finger along the inside corner anyway.

"Handles?" Mara asks.

"Later," the boy says. "Let the runners set."

"Morning tea," someone calls from the back. No one moves.

"Finish the line," Art says.

The boy pares two pins.

At eleven forty-five Mara claps once. The room stops.

The boy wipes his bench with his palm and then the cloth. He wraps the plane in his own tea towel, clumsy.

Art adjusts the fold. "Next week bring the square," he says. "Or borrow mine and return it."

"I'll bring mine," the boy says.

They carry the bedside to the op shop side room. It doesn't wobble. The drawer slides.

Ed signs the tag, satisfied.

At the door the boy hesitates, then holds out his hand. "Thanks," he says. A handshake.

"Keep your knife sharp," Art says.

The boy grins and goes.

Under the awning, Joy waits with one cup. "Home?"

"Home," he says.

At the table he doesn't unwrap the plane. He sets the bag down and leaves it. "He did it," he says.

"He did," she says.

After lunch he goes to the shed and stands in the doorway. He comes back and sits.

Ruth knocks once and leans in with lemons. "Good morning?"

"Handed over," Joy says.

"Best kind," Ruth says.

Dale knocks at two. "Oval?"

"Oval," Art says. On the far side Dale says, "Kid's got hands."

"Hands learn," Art says.

"From someone," Dale says.

"From the wood," Art answers.

In the evening he moves the square to the sideboard and then, after a minute, back into the bag. He rinses a glass and leaves it near enough straight. She leaves it.

Before bed he says, "Next week he won't need telling."

"Good," she says.

"Good," he repeats and turns off the light.

"You turned off the light." She says. "But I'm still here."

"What?"

"You turned off the light."

"Oh."

"Leave it on when I'm still here."

"Oh."

He walks up the stairs, confused. Then says: "Sorry."

She sits. Looks at her hands. Thinks. Turns off the lights. Climbs the stairs well after him, so she doesn't have to see his no-bum.

PART III SPRING

51

On Time

Saturday's light is flat. Her blind page says: *I don't know who I am. I don't know who he is.*

At twelve twenty-eight a Ute at the kerb. Door, boots, gate. Two minutes early. Brendan touches the side wall, says the code once under his breath, doesn't use it. He knocks and waits.

"Come in," she says.

"On time," Art says.

"On time," Brendan answers.

He looks at the sideboard—plane, screws tin.

"Walk?" he asks.

"Short one," Art says. "Oval."

They go. Father and Son. She looks at their backsides. Brendan adjusts to his father's pace. At the corner he keeps the outside so the path is easy. They pass Alan's gate that leaned and does not now. "Spacer," Art says.

"Right," Brendan says.

At the oval they do the long side, not the wet one. A kid practices drop punts and misses cleanly. "Holds its line," Art says.

"Front tyres?" Brendan asks.

"Quiet in the wet," Art says.

"Good," Brendan says.

They sit on the bench halfway and don't try for a talk. "Dale Wednesday two," Art says.

"Good," Brendan says.

Back by one-fifteen. Joy has ham, tomatoes, the right bread. Brendan washes his hands. He cuts the tomatoes. They eat at the table. He places a coaster, map side up: Tasmania. "We should go," he says, testing an old plan.

"Local," Art says.

Brendan grins.

"Code?" Joy asks, halfway through.

Brendan says the numbers. "In my head."

"Good," she says.

After lunch he rinses his plate, gets the rack right the first time. He moves the chair with the fixed leg a thumb's width, then moves it back. "Solid," he says.

"Shim from waste," Art says.

"Waste from what," Brendan asks.

"Fence," Art says.

Brendan nods.

What the hell are they talking about?

At one fifty-five Brendan says, "I'll run the ute," and takes the keys from the bowl with a glance at Art.

"I need my shoes," says Art.

Brendan fetches them, sets them near his father's feet. After the long ritual with the shoes, he opens the door for his father, waits. The engine turns, sounds like it should. They go round the block once, no heroics. Back in five. Keys down.

Two o'clock. "Tea?" Joy asks.

"Got to shoot," Brendan says. "Traffic."

"Go then," she says.

At the step he stops. "Next Saturday?"

"Don't pencil," Joy says.

"I'll come," he says.

Art says the code once more, then the license conditions: "Daylight. Local. Short runs"

"Short runs," Brendan echoes.

Gate. Boots. Ute. Gone.

Inside, the house returns to its two people. Art stands by the sideboard and taps the folder once.

"He was on time," Joy says.

"On time," he agrees.

She writes two lines:

Came with nothing, left nothing to fix.

Code and rules by heart.

He moves the coaster back under his glass, map-side down. She leaves it.

In the evening, he turns off the lights on her again.

Hey, you're doing it again. She doesn't realise she has only thought it, not said.

She climbs the stairs. She runs with wolves that night. She swims with fish. She flies with birds. She is large. She is everywhere. She is a diva with red shoes. She can fly.

52

The Corner

Morning's soft. He says, "Milk," and takes the list with one word on it. Shoes. Wallet. Glasses. Keys from the bowl. "Back in ten."

She opens the notebook. *Contemplate death* it says. *The Buddhists do it. The counsellor said it.*

He turns left after the oval. Blue sign. The detour sign is out again, a new arrow where the old one used to be. He obeys. A street later, another arrow points nowhere. He slows. Two lefts become too many and the houses look strange. The trees do too. He pulls in under a jacaranda that hasn't committed to bloom. He takes the spare map from his wallet, the enlarged one. He unfolds it. Left after the oval points the other way from where his nose is headed. He turns the map, not the car, until the creek line finds his memory. He breathes once and drives slowly to the servo.

Inside, same attendant, new haircut. "You right?"

"Milk," Art says, and sets it on the counter. Then: "Back to the oval?"

"Out, right, over the creek, second left—watch the school zone," the attendant says.

"Second left," Art repeats. He pays, card the right way.

He drives the instructions. Over the creek, slow for the school, second left. The blue hardware sign appears on his right. He doesn't turn. Finally, at the house he parks straight. Ten minutes have become twenty. He lifts the milk and goes to the side wall. He dials the code once, opens, shuts. Inside.

She looks up from the table. "Roadworks?"

"Arrows the wrong way," he says. He places the milk to the left of the juice.

"Arrows," she says. *What am I saying?*

"Servo," he says.

He does not notice when I'm talking nonsense.

Later, she walks to Ruth's with the library notice. Ruth meets her at the gate. "Saw him go past twice," Ruth says, as if reporting weather. "Not worried."

"He went to the servo to ask," Joy says.

"Good radius," Ruth answers. They laugh.

After lunch he takes the Ute to the corner and back. He parks, sets the keys in the bowl.

He opens the cupboard where the map lives and taps it once with two fingers.

Brendan texts: *All good?*

Art types: *Arrows wrong. Servo set me straight.* Sends.

Good self-correct, Brendan replies.

At two, Dale knocks. "Oval?"

"Oval," Art says. They walk the long side. At the far corner Dale says, "Roadworks confusing?"

"The arrows are wrong," Art says.

"Left after the oval," Dale says.

"Still," Art says.

She writes three lines:

Map did its job, not the story.

Servo as waypoint.

Ten minutes became twenty again.

In the evening, he takes the milk out, pours, returns it to the left of the juice, shuts the door. He sets the glass near enough straight. She leaves it. Before bed he stands by the side wall a moment and doesn't open the safe. He touches the eave where the drip line ends. The house, indifferent and kind at the same time, accepts this as routine. She doesn't.

She sits in the dark. Climbs the stairs. Falls in her younger body.

53

Pairs

On her blind page in her notebook it says: *No new words*. A reverse smiley emoji. Mouth corners pointing down. She smiles. *Mankeeper. Mansplaining.*

Len has rang the night before. "Short of a pair for the visit from Moorlands. Friendly. No medals."

Art looks at Joy. She shrugs. "If you want."

"Two hours," Len says. "Tea after."

"Two," Art says.

Whites from the wardrobe door. Hat found without help. They walk in at ten. The green shows seams. Moorlands men stand in a row. Len sets the mat. "Twelve ends, no measure if we can help it," he says. "Keep it moving."

Art picks up his first bowl and holds it until the weight talks back. The line is there. He sends it. It runs long, checks, dies decent.

Len hums.

Moorlands lead puts one close enough to claim it.

Len answers steady.

Art's second narrows and sits. The end goes to them by a hand's width.

Joy stands behind the agapanthus, shade thin. She claps with the rest when clapping is required.

Dale wanders in late, stays by the fence.

Fourth end, Moorlands throw short twice.

Len moves the mat to punish and smiles.

Art finds the length and keeps it. The rink runs fair. Sixth end.

Len reaches, pauses, hands the string to Art.

Art kneels slower than last year, lines the points, breathes. "Yours," he says to Moorlands, clean.

The man nods.

Eighth, a gust lifts collars. It is as if they have butterflies below their chins.

Art's first bowl drifts and dies wrong side. He doesn't fetch it. Second sits useful.

Len's last nicks the jack and leaves it with theirs. "Two," he says.

They agree.

Between ends they don't talk much. Len says "Weight" once.

Art answers: "Green's honest."

A Moorlands skip tries a weighted shot with more hope than plan. It misses and he grins at his own optimism.

Joy takes water to the fence and sets it down.

"Good?" she asks.

"Local," Art says.

Local? Why do I even think this?

Tenth end, Moorlands lead drops a perfect opener.

Len nods, no clap.

Art draws inside it by a coat of paint.

Dale lets a breath out.

Eleventh wants another measure. Len looks at Art. Art reads it. "Ours," he says. He stands slow.

Twelfth is tidy. Hands are shaken.

"Good roll," Moorlands say. "See you next time."

Len pockets the pencil he didn't use.

At the esky Art takes water and returns the cup. He doesn't hover for praise. Len taps his elbow once. "Steady," he says.

Joy folds the picnic chair she hasn't sat in.

Dale comes to the gate. "Clean measure," he says.

"Twice," Art says.

"Twice," Dale agrees.

On the way out they pass the noticeboard. Mixed pairs in a month. Art taps the board with two fingers.

Home by noon. He puts the hat brim up on the peg. He sets the small tin of chalk back in the drawer.

Lunch is ham, tomatoes, the bread with square corners. He eats with the even chew and wipes his mouth and sets the serviette on the plate to signal finished. "Good grass," he says.

"Honest," she says. *Why do we call it honest?*

After, he takes the square from the bag and returns it to the top of the sideboard, then changes his mind and puts it back in the bag.

She writes two lines:

Two measures called clean.

No medals needed.

At two, Dale knocks. "Oval?"

"Oval," Art says. They walk the long side. At the far corner Dale says, "Mixed pairs?"

Art nods.

In the evening he rinses and leaves the glass near enough straight. She leaves it. Spring light hangs on a bit longer.

Before bed he says, "Green was honest."

"It was," she says. *Why do we say honest?*

He leaves her in the dark. He taps the sideboard once as he passes. Her hands seem to give off light. She climbs the stairs in the pitch dark. Almost falls. A surge of adrenaline. *I caught the railing just in time. What if I break a hip first? What if I die first?*

She dies the death that is called sleep. She runs with wolves. She swims with fish. She flies with birds. She is large. She is everywhere. She is a diva with red shoes. She can fly.

54

The Treshold

Her blind page says: *The treshold* for some reason or another Saturday's soft, the windows on the latch.

She moves two chairs under the eaves, tests shade. The table gets a cloth, a centre piece. Coasters out, maps side down. She sets a jug of water with slices of lemon because Ruth brings cordial that stains.

Art checks the back gate hinge with two fingers. "Quiet," he says. He lays the square on the sideboard and then puts it away.

Ruth arrives first with a cake. "Insurance," she says, setting it down. She reads the room like a barometer. Alan follows with a carton of mandarins and a story about a ladder. "Fences hold," he says.

"Braces," Art says.

"Shim from waste," Alan returns, pleased he remembered.

Dale comes at the half-hour with a packet of biscuits and an apology. "Traffic," he says to the garden.

Mara appears. "Boy's late," she says. "He's sanding a runner he miscut and wants to put it right."

Brendan parks at twelve-thirty-two.

Plates. Bread. Ham. Tomatoes. Cake. Ruth pours cordial. Alan cuts the cake with a careful hand. Dale finds the good knife.

Conversation is small, local. Hall. Gates. The oval's south side puddle. A man from the club who cannot find his hat. Someone says "weather".

The boy arrives last, hair clean and damp. He stands in the doorway until invited and then sits on the edge of a chair. "Did you fix it?" Art asks.

"Yes," the boy says.

They eat. Art pours water. He sets coasters under three glasses and misses one; Alan slides his under it.

Dale leans back and says, to no one, "Hinges all quiet."

"Spacers," Art says.

Mara lifts her cup. "To Tuesdays," she says.

"Tuesdays," the boy says.

Ruth folds the cake paper and tucks it under the plate so wind won't get it.

Brendan clears two plates and returns. Joy notes that.

After, they stand in the yard with cups. Alan points at Ruth's lemon tree. "Fruit year," he says.

"Two ticks," Ruth says.

The boy finds the gate and opens and shuts it twice, gentle, listening like he has been taught. He looks in the shed.

"Go in, have a look," Art says.

Dale checks his watch at two. "Oval?" he offers.

"Stay," Joy says. "Tea."

They stay.

Three o'clock slides. People stand. Plates empty, the cloth is not stained. Ruth takes her dish and leaves the lid behind by accident on purpose so she can return for it. Alan takes his car for a run. Mara tells the boy "Tuesday". Art says: "Tuesday" back. Dale says "Wednesday two."

Brendan lingers at the step. "Next week?" he says.

"Don't pencil," Joy says.

"I'll come," he says.

Don't promise.

They go. The yard returns to its usual quiet. The jug goes in the sink.

Art stands under the eaves. "Held," he says.

"It did," she says. *Why do we say held?*

He takes the blue-tied key from the safe and puts it back, tests the code once, closes the door.

Inside, he moves the chair with the good leg a thumb's width back. He sets a coaster map-side up this time.

She writes three lines:

People came with nothing to fix.

Tuesday, Wednesday, Saturday hold.

The gates stayed quiet.

In the evening he eats and rinses and leaves the glass near enough straight. She leaves it. The house hums.

Before bed he says, "Mixed pairs?" without looking at the calendar.

"Let the notice sit," she says.

He nods.

What a weird conversation. Have we always done this?

She sits in his darkness. Her hands glow. She climbs. She falls. She runs with animals.

55

Breakwater

She wakes before the kettle.

Her blind page says: *Weird conversations.* Summer's early. The windows are already on the latch. She sets the lemon mug left of the sink. He comes in, finds the glass without looking, fills it, drinks. He lifts the keys, puts them back. "Daylight's later."

The folder sits on the sideboard, equal distance from the screws tin and the plane. He taps them. The key safe is a square under the eave. He taps it. The map is in the cupboard. He taps its door.

He writes one word on the shopping slip in tidy caps: *oranges.* He leaves the pen parallel.

Oranges again?

Ruth's bin lid clicks once next door, then nothing. A magpie inspects the lawn.

He checks the square in the bag, the small plane wrapped, the old wiper. *Did he fish it from the bin again?*

She sits with the notebook and writes one line: *Enough holds.* Closes it.

He says, "Breakwater?"

"Okay," she says.

They go. They haven't done this in ages. Left after the oval. Blue sign. The path is itself, like it has always been. The water does what water does. Like it always was but different. They stand at the rail. He points, not at anything, then lowers his hand. She names two gulls. They turn for home when the light suggests it. Inside the house he sets his glass near enough straight. She leaves it. He turns off the lights. She sits. Her hands glow. She climbs careful not to fall. She falls anyway. She runs with animals. She expands.

56

Evening

Heat eases. Windows are on the latch. The air is salty. The blind page in her notebook says: *Falling. Running with animals.*

He sits in the good chair with the square edge, hat's on the peg, glass is on the table.

She steps onto the path and clears a strand of spider silk from Ruth's lemon tree with one finger. It breaks cleanly.

Ruth's laugh carries once and stops.

Dale's text arrives with a single word—*Wednesday*—and waits. She does not answer.

He writes *bread* on the slip in tidy caps. Sets the pen a fraction skew, then straightens it.

Light thins. They stand at the back step and watch the lawn invent a colour between green and dark.

She says, "Tomorrow?"

"Local," he says.

We've lost the plot. Completely.

They go inside before the mozzies start. The house closes around them in the ordinary way. Keys are in the bowl. A dog barks in the distance.

How do I stop this? Everything happens by itself. There's nobody who makes this all happen. There's nobody to blame. Everything just happens in its own time. It won't stop. Things are what they are. Kindness is better than rage.

He turns off the lights on her. She cries real tears.

In the morning, she walks the foreshore alone while the air still remembers the dark. The two pelicans at the boat ramp. The runner whose dog keeps to his knee. The woman with the long plait appears at the same bend as always and does not nod. She waits at the shoe shop's door until it opens. She buys the red shoes. They are not high-heeled or even made of leather. It's too late for that. They are a kind of sneaker, but red nevertheless. She takes them off at the door. They stand with the other pairs. He comes to the door and looks at them. Puzzled.

New Words

Ruth and Joy are sitting at Ruth's kitchen table. Ruth's arm is around Joy's shoulder. Joy is summing up all the new words she's learned at the library, at the book club and at the coffee shop.

"Mankeeper. Mansplainer." Ruth howls with laughter.

"Gaslighting. Cancelling. Consent."

"What does these mean?" Ruth asks.

Joy explains.

Ruth says: "It sure would have helped if we knew them words and their meaning."

Joy takes a list from her pocket, unfolds, explains: BAME. Bopo. Bropropriate. Cancel culture. Cis. Cultural appropriation, Fast fashion, Flexitarian. Gender binary. Greenwash. Internalised Misogyny. Intersectionality. Toxic masculinity. Triggers.

Ruth laughs. "You listed them in alphabetical order. So you."

"He's a cis male," says Joy. "Always was, always will be. Here's another one: LGBTQQIP2SAA. It stands for lesbian, gay, bisexual, transgender, queer, questioning, intersex, pansexual, two-spirit, androgynous, and asexual."

"There's a whole world out there," says Ruth, "that we don't know a thing about."

"There is!"

The Animal Poems

Joys sits in the studio, door closed. She feels that, before anything else, she needs to write straight from the heart. Now. Poetry suits. Her fingers touch the keyboard and begin to move.

From the Belly

(The sound of a car approaching)
From this belly wrecked
by baby feet and hunger
beams a feeling to which I must listen
streams a signal that I must catch
eyes closed, breath held, ears alert
what says the belly?
(The sound of a car disappearing in the distance)

Giving Birth to a Stone

For four days it has been sitting there
Giving him the shits
Constipation with a Capital C
It doesn't visit him often but when it does
It occupies him fully, until he has a double shot of coffee
In his Capuchino at the library café
And he must run to the double-U C
To give birth to a stinking stone
(the sound of a stone falling in a lake)

What a Strange Night

(The sound of an ultrasound detecting a heartbeat)
What strange songs came to mind last night
These poems from the underworld
where old pain lives and freedom from
where baby animals are born
amid organ, blood, slime, and bone
where a throbbing orchestra plays melodies
unknown, dark and bacterial
where wet things are packed tightly
wrapped in orange peel and trapped air
Unfinished on purpose
(The sound of an ultrasound detecting a heartbeat)

The Call of a Child

(The beams of car lights passing move over the ceiling, a dog
barks in the distance)
My middle-aged son dissolves . . .
A visiting child cries: Mam! Mahaaaam!
My mother heart jumps
My entire vein network becomes alive
Once I was *mam*, now my empty arms ache
Will death be a refilling of arms, a replenishing of heart
or a prolonged sharp cry
for *mam*?
(The beams of car lights passing move over the ceiling)

Ruth

(Street noise in the background, the smell of fresh coffee)
You were so easy to get to know
so approachable, so kind
So much fun to be with
You knock and lean
You are so easy to love, so light
is your footprint upon the earth
You made soup for months
When I was sick or he was

You are so easy to leave
You make sandwiches and store
bottles of well water in the Ute
You are so easy to miss
I don't think of you. It is as if
You are everywhere
(Street noise in the background, a group of women in hijab pass-
ing)

The Mankeeper

(A radio playing in the distance, sounds of someone cooking)
She is the keeper of a yes-but man
She thinks she is too old to leave him
She researches his various ailments
While he suffers wordlessly but loudly
Void of curiosity, full of victimhood
She accompanies him to his appointments
Between his bouts of TV
She acts like a saint but inside
The mankeeper burns with fury and disdain
While he resents her constant interference
with his diet, his victimhood, his brain fog
(A radio playing in the distance, sounds of someone cooking)

She leans back in her chair and reads what she wrote. She titles it: *The Animal Poems.*

She starts a blank file. She titles it: *The Mankeeper.* She looks at her notes. Her fingers begin to type:

At seventy-nine, Joy has a new job title. It sits under her skin like a splinter: *Mankeeper.* She learned this word yesterday and knows it fits her like a glove. No, she's not dressing him, not bathing him. Yet. Those will come later, winter weather promised in the forecast. He's not sick. She is not a carer. *He's just old.*

For now, it is the invisible work that takes her breath. She reads his face the way farmers look at the sky and decide on the day. High cloud means caution. A heat haze means slowness. A crisp blue can still deliver a gust that knocks a person sideways. She keeps the kettle ready and the voice she uses for mornings, a shade brighter than her own.

The house carries the habits of their marriage. Shoes aligned by the back door. Tea towels folded precisely, one on the oven rail. The lawn kept short. The clothes in the cupboards, pressed, steamed. Simple nutritious meals in the freezer. Dust kept at bay. A favourite mug with a crack that lengthens filament by filament. . .

About the book

At seventy-nine, Joy learns a new word: Mankeeper. The word fits
and chafes at once. In a coastal town of bowls greens, church pews
and Norfolk pines, she tends to Art in the realm where care is mostly
invisible, reading the weather of his face, staging days with lists and
small calibrations, keeping pills lined up next to plates and hope
tucked under a fridge magnet. As seasons turn, a fall on the back
step, a neighbour's kindness, a son's visits, and the camaraderie of a
men's tools shed rearrange the household barometers of rage and de-
pendence.

Rendered in exacting, luminous detail, *The Mankeeper* is a close-
up portrait of late-life partnership, how love, habit and stubborn au-
tonomy jostle in kitchen and shed, on the breakwater and under the
eave. It is about the choreography of ageing, the politics of chores
and tone, and the audacity of claiming an hour to write. Joy is small
and grand at once, author inside, list-maker outside, learning what
is hers to carry and what she can set down. In sentences as steady as
a hand on a shoulder, this book asks what it means to keep another
safely in the world without losing oneself.

The Mankeeper

© Suzanne Visser

Published by Clear Mind Press, 2025, in Alice Springs, Australia

ISBN Print: 978-1-7643393-0-8

EISBN Ebook: 978-1-7643393-1-5

Typeset: Clear Mind Press

Cover Photo: PublicDomainPictures PixaBay

Cover design: Clear Mind Press

Portrait of the author: Hazel Blake

All rights reserved. Except as permitted under the Australian Copyright Act 1968 (for example, fair dealing for study, research, criticism or review), no part of this book may be reproduced, stored in a retrieval system, communicated or transmitted in any form or by any means without prior written permission.

All inquiries should be made to the publisher: info@clearmindpress.com

https://www.clearmindpress.com

Suzanne Visser

Suzanne H Visser (born 1957) is an Australia-based legal scholar, author and publisher. She is the founder and chief executive of Clear Mind Press in Central Australia and the managing director of Sustainable Justice Australia, where her work focuses on sustainable justice, criminal justice systems and space law. Her current scholarship builds practical evaluation tools for law, policy and procedure, developed over extended research periods at Charles Darwin University and the University of Newcastle. She writes and publishes in English after an earlier career in Dutch.

Visser's bibliography spans fiction, non-fiction and poetry. Earlier Dutch-language titles include the thriller *De Vismoorden* (later published in translation as *The Fish Murders*), the novels *Terra Nostra* and *Een man met mooie benen*, and the children's book *De Verdwijning*. Her recent English-language works include the two-volume inquiry *The Elephant's Tooth* (on crime in Alice Springs and rural Australia), *Marks on Paper: Essays on Drawing, Seeing and Looking*, *Never Retire: An Exploration of Old Age*, and *Hundred Fifty Five Sonnets*. As a publisher, she has commissioned and edited a diverse list of authors across essays, memoir, poetry and visual arts.

Visser has lived in Central Australia since 2000. Her practice is shaped by long engagement with embodied disciplines and the arts, including formative periods in Japan, and by sustained work at the intersection of research and community consultation. Across her roles as scholar, writer and publisher, she aims to connect careful inquiry with usable frameworks for institutions and readers alike.

Short stories: *De pracht van het dagelijks leven*; 1991, Bert Bakker (The Glory of Daily Life)

Thriller: *De Vismoorden*; Atlas Uitgeverij, 2000; published in German as *Das Japanische Rätsel*, DVA, 2001; in French as *Les Meurtres au Poisson*, Noir sur Blanc, 2002; in Spanish as *Sushi*, Ediciones B., 2003; in English as *The Fish Murders*, Clear Mind Press, 2022

Children's book: De Verdwijning, Leopold, 2005 (Vanishing)

Novel: *Terra Nostra*, Bookhost, 2003

Novel: *Een man met mooie benen*, Mistral, 2006 (A Bloke With Beautiful Legs

Non-fiction: *I, Unborn, Undying (a Search for the Self)*, For a Clear Mind, 2016

Non-fiction: *The Elephant's Tooth, Crime in Alice Springs*, Clear Mind Press 2022

The Elephant's Tooth, Crime in Rural Australia, Clear Mind Press 2022

Fiction, under pen name Shan: The Carpetbaggers of Mbantua, Clear Mind Press 2022

Non-fiction: *Marks on Paper, Essays on drawing, seeing and looking,* Clear Mind Press 2023

Fictional memoir, under pen name Shan: Women! 1. *Crying Mothers*

Women! 2. The Spirit of the Fox

Women! 3. Journey to the Edge, Clear Mind Press 2023

Non-fiction: *Never Retire, an exploration of old age,* Clear Mind Press 2023

Fiction: *Cash!* Clear Mind Press 2024

Poetry: *Hundred Fifty Five Sonnets,* Clear Mind Press 2025

Non-Fiction: *The Great Kitschification,* Clear Mind Press 2025

Non-Fiction: *Find Your iKiGAi,* Clear Mind Press 2025

Non-Fiction: *Life Force,* Clear Mind Press 2025

www.ingramcontent.com/pod-product-compliance
Lightning Source LLC
Chambersburg PA
CBHW040526170726
48295CB00012B/355